DIAMO

If there was a more overbearing,
thoroughly disagreeable man than Nick
Diamond, Sherril had never met him—
and he lived in darkest Yorkshire! Yet for
the sake of her beloved father Sherril had
not only had to uproot herself from
London but was having to work—no,
slave—for Nick as well. How could she
stand it?

DIAMOND STUD

BY

MARGARET MAYO

MILLS & BOON LIMITED
15-16 BROOK'S MEWS
LONDON W1A 1DR

First published 1981
Australian copyright 1981
Philippine copyright 1982
This edition 1982

© Margaret Mayo 1981

ISBN 0 263 73996 1

Set in Monophoto Baskerville 11 on 12½ pt.
05–1082

Made and printed in Great Britain by
Richard Clay (The Chaucer Press) Ltd,
Bungay, Suffolk

CHAPTER ONE

SHERRIL sighed and changed position for the hundredth time.

Her father glanced across and smiled. 'Only a few more miles. If you want to stop and stretch your legs we can, but I'd prefer to press on. I'd like to be there before dark.'

There was no answering smile on Sherril's face. She would have liked to stop, to put off the moment when they arrived at Weirbrook, but rather than upset her father she shook her head. 'I'll survive.'

But each yard seemed like a mile, each mile like ten. It was all right for her father, he had a new and exciting job to look forward to. She had been compelled to give up her own job and say goodbye to all her friends. How was she likely to find another one in the wilds of Yorkshire?

She did not share Peter Martin's love of horses, could not understand why he had wanted to change from his safe steady work at a stables not too far away from their home.

No, that was not true, she did know the reason. The death of her mother had left him bewildered and unhappy and he wanted to get away from the memories.

A new start, a new life, he had said. She had not thought he meant it until he informed her that he had been offered a wonderful job in a stud in

Yorkshire where the owner was well known to him.

He had asked her opinion, said he would not go unless she was in full agreement. But he had been so keen, so eager, for the first time since her mother died, that Sherril had not had the heart to say no.

They said it was more easy to adapt when you were young. She hoped it was true. She had lived within easy reach of London all her twenty-one years, had loved the night life. There was always something to do, somewhere to go.

She was going to miss all that. What was there to do in the Yorkshire Dales? Precisely nothing, she guessed, and let out another unconscious sigh. And then, seeing her father's lips tighten, she touched his arm. 'I'm sorry, I know I shouldn't feel like this, but I can't help it. I'll be all right once we're there.'

He held her hand a moment. 'I imagine there'll be plenty of people your own age, sons and daughters of local farmers. You won't be bored for long.'

'You're probably right,' she said, and resumed her surveillance of the grassy fells. She caught occasional glimpses of a river as it wound its way along the valleys, the intricate pattern of drystone walls climbing up hill and down dale in endless procession.

Only occasionally did they see signs of habitation, stone farmhouses and tiny cottages, each with its surrounding patch of cultivated earth.

She reached into her handbag and took out a comb. Her green eyes glared back at her from the mirror on the sun visor, startling her. Take a grip, she scolded herself, things might not be all that bad.

Her honey-blonde hair waved carelessly about her

heart-shaped face. She was a pretty girl, an only child, and although she had been spoilt to a certain extent she had an appealing personality and had never found it difficult to make friends.

She put away her comb and settled back into her seat. 'Is Mr Diamond married?' she enquired, thinking perhaps he might have a family nearer her own age.

Peter Martin shrugged. 'I have no idea. I've met him purely in the line of business. He's a tough man, that much I know, but very fair. I'm confident I shall like working for him.'

Sherril wished she was as confident of being happy. The nearer they got the more uneasy she became. She wondered what her father would say if she suggested going back to London. He did not approve of girls living alone in the big city, had voiced his opinion on that many times, yet she knew he would not want her to be unhappy.

They arrived at Weirbrook, a huddle of houses built out of local stone. A few children played by the roadside, an old man wearing a cloth cap leaned against a wall, a clay pipe dangling from one corner of his mouth. A dog lay in the middle of the road, making no attempt to move even though he saw their approaching car.

Peter Martin stopped, called out to the old man, 'Can you tell me where the Diamond place is, please?'

Pale eyes looked at him curiously, but the obvious questions were not asked. He lifted a bent arm and pointed with his pipe. 'Up t' road another mile, turn left, you'll see sign.'

Sherril's father nodded his thanks and slid the car into gear. Still the dog lay there. He sounded his horn with no result. Not until the old man called him did the dog move, and then it was with reluctance.

Peter smiled. 'I guess this is the way of life up here. No one's in a hurry. Not like the rat race we've left behind. I'm glad to be out of it.'

Sherril said nothing, watching the road in front without interest, noting that when they turned off the main track the landscape appeared even more barren.

Suddenly the land fell away before them. In a wide valley lay the Diamond stud, a conglomeration of solid grey stone buildings which was to be their home for the next goodness knows how long.

Sherril looked at them dispassionately. The place was as bad as she had thought, in the middle of nowhere, no other houses in sight. The future did not look good.

Her father on the other hand sat forward eagerly scanning the building. 'What a place! It's magnificent!'

It was certainly big, she would grant him that. Apart from the house, which was of massive proportions, there appeared to be dozens of outbuildings, stables, sheds, barns, as well as several cottages which she presumed were occupied by the men who worked for Mr Diamond.

They were to live in one of them. According to her father, the man whose position he was to replace had worked for both Mr Diamond and his father before him.

They drove into the yard, but apart from a black and

white terrier there was no one about. Sherril climbed from the car and stretched her arms above her head.

'What a welcome,' she said bitterly, 'after we've driven over two hundred miles. Are you sure he was expecting you today?'

'I should imagine Mr Diamond has far better things to do than hang around for us,' replied her father, stretching too, and looking about him with interest. 'My, I'm going to like working here.'

He walked over to the stables where a single head glanced inquisitively in their direction. 'And what's wrong with you, my beauty? Why have they left you here on your own?'

The bay mare licked his palm, sensing a friend, but when Sherril approached her ears went back and a wary expression crossed her face.

Her father smiled ruefully. 'Horses can tell when you're frightened. You'll have to get over your fears, living here. Horses will be the main form of transport.'

Sherril said nothing, knowing her father was disappointed she did not share his love of equine animals. But she could not help it. Her limp was a constant reminder of the brute who had thrown her when she was first learning to ride, and nothing or no one would ever get her on horseback again.

She looked over her shoulder. 'I think there's someone coming.'

The man who approached was like no one she had seen before. Her first impression was of tremendous height and a powerful physique, carrying himself with an air of authority. It had to be Mr Diamond.

Her father held out his hand, smiling. 'Mr Diamond, nice to see you again. This is my daughter, Sherril.'

'Glad you made it.' The big man's voice seemed to come from somewhere in his stomach.

He gave Sherril no more than a cursory glance before turning his attention back to her father. 'We certainly need you, Peter. Bring your car, I'll show you your living quarters.'

They followed him down a lane which curved away from the stable yard. It was no more than a hundred yards to the tiny cottage, and its neglected appearance caused Sherril's spirits to drop even further.

Her father opened the boot and his new employer picked up the two cases as though they were empty, tucking a box under each arm. Peter Martin took the remaining cases from the back seat and Sherril her own bits and pieces.

She decided she did not like Mr Diamond, eyeing him rebelliously as he kicked open the door with a booted foot, dropping their cases inside. He was rude. He had not even bothered to say hello to her, nor ask what sort of journey they had had.

'If you come with me, Peter,' he rumbled, 'I'll show you around.'

'What about me?' demanded Sherril, unable to contain her growing anger. 'What am I supposed to do?'

Cool grey eyes turned on her. Unnerving eyes, see through you eyes. 'Unpack, of course. Get your father a meal. Isn't that what you're here for?'

Too stupefied to do more than stare, Sherril turned her attention to her father, expecting him to suggest she accompany them on their tour of the farm.

But Peter Martin surprisingly agreed with Mr Diamond. 'That's right, Sherry,' he said. 'I don't know about you, but I'm starving. See what you can fix.'

Sherril flounced inside angrily. She had expected Mr Diamond to have a meal waiting for them, on this their first day, not leave them to fend for themselves. He was unsociable, to say the least. She wondered whether he was married, whether his wife was of the same calibre. God help them if she was.

The room in which she found herself was tiny, the furniture old and decrepit, of no great value, and the whole covered with a film of dust. The windows were grimy and let in little light, the curtains stiff with dirt.

She shuddered and moved through into the kitchen, not surprised to find it in the same filthy state.

And Mr Diamond expected her to cook a meal in it! What sort of man was he?

Without stopping to think Sherril limped out of the cottage after the two men who stood talking in the stable yard. Always impulsive, she tapped her father's new employer on his arm.

'I refuse to live in that dirty cottage! Why hasn't someone got it ready for us? What do you think we are, pigs, to be shoved into a sty like that?'

Her father's face turned from a healthy pink to a deep embarrassed red. 'Sherril! Please don't talk to Mr Diamond like that. I'm sure he——'

He stopped when he saw Mr Diamond's face.

Sherril received the full blast of his icy stare, his silver eyes shooting her down so that she stepped back a pace before she even realised what she was doing.

'You're a healthy young female, aren't you?' Insolent eyes looked her up and down, taking in the smart new suit she had worn to travel in, the crisp white blouse and elegant suede shoes. 'I suggest you change into something more suitable and get on with it. No one here has time to go cleaning cottages.'

Incensed by his manner, by the way he had looked at her body as though it lacked something, Sherril flared, 'Who keeps your house clean? Your wife, your housekeeper? Couldn't she have done it?'

'Really, Sherril!' interrupted her father.

But Sherril was past caring, glaring hostilely at the big man, who stared at her as though she were a nobody, a nuisance come to try him.

Silver eyes narrowed until they were mere slits. He took a deep breath and seemed to grow in stature by several more inches, towering above her. Had she not been angry she would have been terrified.

When he spoke, it was quietly, and she scarcely caught the words. 'I suggest you go back and get on with it if your father wishes to keep his job. I had no idea he had a wayward daughter like you.'

Despite the softness there was a hidden threat. Sherril gave him one last defiant stare before turning. She knew how much this job meant to her parent, she could not let him down. But even so it was difficult to refrain from muttering beneath her breath, 'Bigheaded, arrogant swine, I hope I don't run into you too often!'

She had not thought he heard, not until a heavy
hand clamped her shoulder. 'Young lady, I'd be
careful what you say, if I were you. I'll give you fair
warning, I'm not an easy man to get on with at the
best of times, but if anyone gets on the wrong side of
me, as you seem intent on doing, then by heavens
they know it.'

His hand was like a sledgehammer, weighing her
down, hurting, irritating. 'Since you're not my employer, I can speak to you how I like,' she returned
defiantly. 'There's not much you can do about it.'

'No?' A thick black brow rose caustically. 'Carry
on like this and you'll find out. I have no time for
complaining women. They have a job in life and I
expect them to get on with it.'

'My God, the original male chauvinist!' cried
Sherril, wrenching herself free, her green eyes flash-
ing fire. 'Hasn't anyone ever told you about
Women's Lib?'

She was vaguely aware of her father on the edge
of this scene, wringing his hands, his face pale now
with apprehension. But she was certainly not going
to let this man put her down. Who did he think he
was?

Grey eyes blazed with equal intensity. 'I've no
time for liberated woman,' he said, 'not unless they
pull their weight. Seems to me that's what you should
be doing, helping your father get settled instead of
creating a scene that's doing nothing but harm.'

'That's right, Sherril,' added her father anxiously.
'You go and see to the cottage. I'll give you a hand
as soon as I'm through.'

'You won't have time,' said Mr Diamond tersely. 'Let the girl get on with it, it will do her good.'

Sherril breathed out savagely and how she refrained from answering back she did not know. Only by exercising maximum control over her enraged feelings did she manage to turn and walk back to the cottage.

She heard her father say, 'I'm sorry, Mr Diamond. She's not usually like that. It must be the long journey.'

The big man's reply was lost to her as she slammed the door in a last gesture of defiance. How could her father grovel? Surely he did not agree that she was in the wrong?

And as for him expecting them to live here! It was unbelievable. She did not even know where to begin. The whole house wanted a thorough spring-clean. It would take a day to get rid of the top dirt, and it was tea time already, and they had had a long journey, and she was tired—and oh, she wished they were back in London!

She sat down heavily on a wooden chair and then sprang up immediately, realising that she had most probably soiled her new suit. 'Damn!' she said aloud. 'Damn, damn, damn!'

She wandered upstairs and the situation did not improve. The two bedrooms, filled with ugly furniture, were thick with dust, and smelled musty as though they had been closed for many months.

With a struggle Sherril managed to open the windows and then tugging up one of the cases changed into a pair of jeans and a sleeveless tee-shirt. The only consolation was that at least the mattresses on the beds were new, still in their polythene wrappings. Someone had been here, so why hadn't they cleaned the place, or at least made arrangements for someone else to do it?

Sherril felt nauseated by it all and it made matters worse when she could find no cleaning materials, and the only broom was minus most of its bristles.

There was only one thing for it, she decided mutinously. She would go up to Mr Diamond's house and demand that they supply her with the necessary equipment.

A thought no sooner had to cross Sherril's mind than she acted on it, and a few seconds later she walked determinedly along the path that led to the big house.

It was of solid Yorkshire stone, as were all the buildings she had seen since coming to this part of the country, and looked well cared for; windows gleaming, paintwork shining, flower garden neatly tended.

This obvious care strengthened Sherril's animosity and she banged on the door impatiently, words already tumbling to her lips. But although she knocked several times, and rang the bell continuously, no one came to see who was causing the commotion.

She was tempted to try the door, find for herself the utensils she required, but a picture of Mr Diamond flitted before her mind's eye, tall, forbidding, totally aggressive, and she weakened.

More slowly now, she returned to the cottage. She had been inside for no more than a few seconds when someone knocked. No use trying to wonder who it might be.

It was a relief to see a friendly face. A woman only a few years older than herself smiled warmly. 'Hello, I'm Meg Rowbotham, my husband's one of the stud hands. You must be Mrs Martin, you're younger than I imagined.'

'Miss Martin—Sherril.' She stood back for the other woman to enter. 'Am I pleased to see you!'

Meg stepped inside and her mouth fell open. 'Crikey, I had no idea! You poor thing, you can't live here.'

Sherril shrugged. 'Try telling that to Mr Diamond. I've just had one hell of a row with him.'

Meg's brown eyes widened. 'That won't do you much good. I should imagine he told you where to get off.'

Reluctantly Sherril nodded. 'If it wasn't for my father, I'd have gone back where I came from. Of all the bigheaded, conceited, arrogant—*pigs*!'

Meg laughed. 'It won't get you anywhere, calling him names. Mr Diamond's word is law about this place, and the sooner you realise it the better.'

'If he thinks I'm going to kowtow to him, he's mistaken,' threatened Sherril 'My father might work for him, but I don't, and no one's going to tell me what to do.'

The other woman shook her head warningly. 'When you're on his property the Diamond law applies to you too. Ease up, Sherril, he's not all that bad. Come on, I'll give you a hand to lick this place into some sort of shape.'

Meg fetched buckets and mops and dusters and polish from her own cottage, and two hours later they had got rid of most of the dirt.

'I don't know how to thank you,' said Sherril when they finally stood back to survey their handiwork.

'A cup of tea will do fine,' said Meg, wiping the back of her hand across her perspiring brow, streaking it with more dirt.

Sherril could not help laughing. 'Don't we look a sight! What wouldn't I give for a good hot bath? But I suppose I'll have to do with a wash down in the sink.'

It had appalled her when she realised the cottage had no bathroom—and that big house up there shrieking of money. It made her livid.

'You and your father must come round and spend an evening with us,' said Meg at once. 'Jack's fixed me up a shower, you can use that. I know it's not the same as a long hot soak, but it's far healthier, so they say.' She sounded as though she was convincing herself.

'Thanks,' said Sherril, filling the kettle, 'anything to get rid of this grime. I've never been so dirty in my life. I can't understand why Mr Diamond didn't get it ready for us.'

'I don't suppose he knew what it was like,' said Meg. 'He's too busy to keep a check on his cottages.'

Sherril tossed her head scornfully. 'Don't make excuses, Meg. He couldn't care less, if the truth's known.'

Meg smiled to herself and shook her head, as if

realising the futility in trying to persuade Sherril otherwise. 'At least the bulk of the work's done. Another week and you'll look back on this and laugh.'

Sherril doubted that. Anything less amusing she had yet to come across.

They sipped their tea and then Meg said she must go. 'I don't want to keep Jack waiting for his evening meal. But don't forget,' she added, 'come over afterwards, we'll be expecting you.'

Left alone, Sherril hunted through their groceries and when her father returned had a meal of sorts waiting.

Peter Martin looked approvingly about him. 'You've worked marvels! I never expected to see it clean so quickly. I'm sorry I let you in for all this, Sherry. It's just one of those things, I suppose, not much we could do about it.'

'We could have, if you'd sided with me,' said Sherril heatedly, thoughts of the Diamond man returning with increased intensity. 'He had no right expecting us to live here. He could at least have had the place cleaned up.'

Her father rested his hand on her shoulder. 'And you had no right speaking to him like you did, Sherril. He's my boss, you know. What would we have done if he'd told us to go? This is our home now and you must learn to make the best of it. Fortunately he put down your temper to the long journey. Just make sure you don't speak to him like that again.'

'I won't speak to him, full stop,' said Sherril

bitterly. 'The only thing I'm thankful for is that *I* don't have to work for him. We'd never see eye to eye, not in a thousand years.'

Her father looked embarrassed, and Sherril's eyes narrowed suspiciously. 'Is there something you haven't told me?'

Peter Martin nodded slowly. 'I've more or less promised Mr Diamond that you'll help out.'

'The devil I will! I can't stand the man. What did you tell him that for?' Highly indignant, Sherril's face burned with unusual colour.

'It was all fixed before we came here. I thought you'd need something to do.' He touched her arm. 'It's for the best, Sherry. You admitted on the way up that you weren't looking forward to life in the Dales.'

'Why didn't you tell me?' demanded Sherril.

'Because I knew how you'd react,' replied her father patiently.

'Too true,' muttered Sherril. 'What is this work I'm supposed to be doing?'

Peter Martin shrugged. 'I don't know, Mr Diamond merely said that he'd find you something to do.'

And after their explosive first meeting Sherril could imagine that it would be anything but enjoyable.

She joined her father at the table in the tiny cramped kitchen which jutted out at the back of the cottage, evening sunlight trying to filter in through the filmy windows.

Peter bit into a sausage, staring thoughtfully at

the remainder left on his fork. 'He's not a bad man, not when you know him. He certainly knows his job, breeds some of the finest racehorses in the country. It must be as difficult for him having to take on someone new, as it is for us. Bert Jenkins had been with him all his life, he knew more about horses than Mr Diamond, even. It was a sad day for the Diamond stud when he died.'

'And it's a sad day for us today,' snapped Sherril. 'Let's change the subject. I'm sick to death of hearing about Mr Diamond. I had a visitor, Meg Rowbotham, she's invited us round this evening.'

'Jack's wife?' Her father looked pleased. 'I was introduced to Jack, seems a decent sort. In fact they're a jolly good crowd altogether. I think moving up here was the best thing I've ever done—apart from marrying your mother, of course.' He looked sad for a moment. 'She wouldn't have liked it here. A proper townie, was your mother. No amount of persuading on my part would make her leave Romford. You're like her, prefer to be within shouting distance of London.'

'You'd hankered to move away before?' asked Sherril, surprised. Her father had always seemed happy in their little suburban home, she had never realised he had wanted anything more.

'I was brought up in the country, remember. I always wanted to go back, but I loved your mother too much to make her do anything she didn't want to do.'

Sherril was silent as they finished their meal. This was a side to her father she had not known, and she

admired him for it. She doubted whether she herself
would be able to survive years and years in an en-
vironment which was not entirely to her liking.

Like the one in which they found themselves now,
for instance. She knew without a shadow of doubt
that she would not be able to live here indefinitely.
It would drive her round the bend.

Her father helped her wash up and then Sherril
said, 'Let's go over to Meg's. I'm not doing any more
work tonight.'

He smiled. 'Give them time to finish their meal,
Sherry love. There's no great rush.'

'There is so far as I'm concerned,' said Sherril.
'She's promised I can use their shower. I feel such a
mess. The sooner you get one fixed up the better.'

'There's no bathroom?' Peter Martin looked surprised. He had not yet had a good look round. 'I'm
sorry, if I'd known——'

'It's not your fault,' cut in Sherril quickly, 'don't
worry, I'll manage.'

An hour earlier she would not have said that, but
hearing how her father had put up with living in
Romford for the past twenty-five years she felt she
could put up without a bathroom, for a week or two
at least.

What infuriated her more than anything was the
fact that that Diamond man must have known what
this place was like, yet he'd let them walk into it
without so much as an apology. In fact he had
seemed to think it her duty to scrub the place clean.

How she hated him!

Their evening at the Rowbothams' put Sherril into

a much better frame of mind. Jack Rowbotham was a bluff Yorkshireman with a keen sense of humour and before long had Sherril in fits of laughter.

It was quite clear, however, that he respected Nicholas Diamond, and none of the anecdotes that he related ever concerned his boss. Indeed when he mentioned him, his tone became almost reverent.

'You couldn't work for a better man, Peter,' he said. 'He's fair and honest and pays a good wage for a good day's work.'

Meg grinned at her visitor. 'Sherril wouldn't say he was fair. The poor girl started off on the wrong foot. I don't expect he'll forgive her easily.'

This was all the encouragement she needed, thought Sherril gloomily. It wouldn't have mattered had her father not let her in for it, by suggesting that she work for Nicholas Diamond. She could have ignored him. But now she was not looking forward to their next encounter and would have preferred not to have him brought into the conversation.

'Nick's all right,' said Jack. 'He won't harbour a grudge. By tomorrow he'll have forgotten all about his cross words. You see if I'm right.'

His wife did not look so sure, and Sherril was more inclined to agree with her. But she tossed her head nonchalantly. 'It doesn't matter to me what he says. So long as Daddy is happy in his work that's all I care about.'

Peter Martin glanced at his daughter proudly. 'We'll both be happy,' he said softly. 'I'll make sure of that.'

Sherril did not sleep easily. Lying in bed in the

little stark room that had nothing in the way of home comforts, she went over and over the events of the day, her meeting with Nick Diamond uppermost in her mind.

He really was the most disagreeable man she had ever met. She had no doubt that he was difficult to work for, demanding and expecting perfection. Fair and honest, Jack had said. That might be, but no doubt his fairness was tempered with a fanatic desire to achieve the impossible, and honesty could mean that he was not averse to telling people a few home truths if he thought they deserved it.

Look how he had spoken to her, as though she was a scrubbing maid, with no thought at all for her feelings. She clenched her teeth in the darkness. Why had her father ever agreed to her working for him. He must have known what he was like, known that they would never hit it off.

For several hours Sherril lay there, listening to the silence. There was no rumble of traffic here, nothing apart from the occasional call of an owl, the distant murmuring of a tumbling beck. Noises of the night that were so much a part of the Dales, yet were strange to Sherril's unaccustomed ears.

It took the rest of the week for her and Meg to put the cottage into order. The curtains had disintegrated when washed, so Meg had lent her some of her own spare ones until Sherril could get into one of the larger towns and purchase the necessary material.

Her father settled down in his new job and spoke with enthusiasm of Mr Diamond, or Nick, as he now

called him. 'Why don't you come and have a look at
the horses?' he asked his daughter many times.
'You'll love the foals, I'm sure. No one could resist
them, not even you.'

'When I have time,' Sherril had demurred,
reluctant to give an outright no, but not wishing to
hurt her father by flatly refusing. A horse was a horse
to her, whether it was a few months old foal or one
of the mares from which Nick bred, and in her eyes
all horses were dangerous animals, best kept well
clear of.

So far she had not had time to get bored with life
in the Dales, her days had been filled with scrubbing
and polishing, washing and ironing, and each night
she had fallen into bed too tired to even think.

But at the beginning of the second week, when
the cottage was restored to order, and was clean and
habitable, if not as comfortable as the house they
had left behind, time began to pall.

Sherril had travelled no farther than the village
shop in Weirbrook, where she had ordered groceries
and cleaning materials, and light bulbs and pegs,
which were delivered by a whistling errand boy on a
bicycle.

Once or twice she and Meg had gone walking,
exploring the surrounding countryside, but Sherril
had no interest and had always been first to suggest
returning.

Now she felt on edge, irritable because she was
penned in without any means of transport to get her
to York or Harrogate. She saw little of her father,
which made matters worse; he was always busy with

the foals, or the mares, up early and often not coming in until it was dark, which meant it was almost time for bed.

She wished now that she had learned to drive when her father suggested it a few years earlier. But she was selfconscious of her limp, slight though it was, and had always claimed that she would never be able to drive.

As a child she had used her limp many times to get her own way and, more often than not, her parents had given in. Now she wished she had not been so prickly about it, because if she had learned to drive she could have used her father's car to get away from this godforsaken place.

There was only one thing to be thankful for, and that was that the odious Nick Diamond had not come anywhere near her again. Perhaps he had changed his mind about her working for him. She sincerely hoped so, because if anything could be worse than sitting here with nothing to do, it would be working for him.

The warm June sunshine had enticed her outside, and wearing nothing more than a pair of brief shorts and a suntop Sherril lay on a blanket spread on the overgrown square of lawn at the back of the house.

A curlew called overhead, a skylark sang his song, in the distance sheep complained and the young foals called to their mothers. She was getting used to the sounds of the countryside, though she knew she could never accept them.

She was like her mother, she supposed, the excitement of town life was born and bred into her. It had been a mistake, really, coming here with her father, though she was prepared to give him a year or two of her life, for the sake of his happiness.

After that, who knew? She might meet Mr Right and get married, or perhaps move on to pastures new. Even in York itself it would not be too bad, and she would be near enough to visit her father. She could even learn to drive, maybe buy herself a car. There were all sorts of possibilities, but that was in the future. At the moment she had to accept the way of life here. She loved her father dearly and no way did she want to make him unhappy by showing her own hatred of this place.

Some sixth sense suddenly told her she was not alone. Only Meg would intrude on her privacy. She smiled and pushed herself up on one elbow, shading her eyes.

But it was not the slim figure of the other woman that greeted her, but a dark male shadow who, from her recumbent position, appeared taller and broader than she remembered.

'What do you want?' she asked sharply.

'I could ask what you are doing,' he snapped. Khaki jodhpurs clung to his muscular thighs, a check shirt stretched across wide shoulders. There was a strength about him, a physical power that was menacing.

Sherril scrambled to her feet and faced him indignantly. 'Isn't it obvious?'

'Quite,' he agreed, 'but I understood from your father that there were jobs in the cottage that were keeping you inordinately busy. Hence the reason I haven't staked my claim on your time. Do I take it that all your work is now finished?'

There was definite unfriendliness in his grey eyes and Sherril felt her blood run cold. This man spelt trouble, no matter that everyone else appeared to have nothing but good to say of him.

Sherril lifted her slim shoulders, green eyes flashing. 'I've done my best.'

'But it's not quite the palatial residence to which you've been accustomed?'

The accuracy of his remark astonished her, made her even more angry. 'If you knew its failings why didn't you do something about it?'

His rugged face was remote, accusing. 'Most of my employees are grateful for a roof over their heads. What they do inside is up to them.'

Sherril clenched her fists. 'You're the most unfeeling man I've ever met, I'm surprised you get anyone to work for you!'

With an impatient gesture he thrust his fingers through his short dark hair. 'Miss Martin, I didn't invite you here. I employed your father, and against my better judgment agreed to find you work as well. If you wish to remain I suggest you at least be civil.'

She returned his gaze steadily. 'If you insist on rubbing me up the wrong way, Mr Diamond, there's nothing I can do about it. It seems to me that the best thing we can do is keep well away from each other.'

'On a place this size?' Thick brows rose sceptically. 'Impossible. More especially when you're working in the stables.'

'In the stables?' Sherril was aghast. 'What is it

you're expecting me to do?'

'The usual thing that any stud hand does,' he said calmly. 'Muck out, sweep the yard, make sure the whole place is clean and tidy.'

'Like hell I will!' snapped Sherril in sudden desperation. 'In case my father hasn't told you, I hate horses, and anything to do with them, I came here because it was what my father wanted.'

He expressed disbelief. 'I can't believe that you're such a dutiful daughter.'

She snatched up the blanket and began folding it, anything to keep her hands off this hateful man. She felt like clawing him, dragging her nails down his face, knowing she would derive full satisfaction from seeing telltale streaks of blood.

'I love my father,' she said heatedly. 'But I don't suppose a man such as you would understand. I doubt you have an ounce of compassion in your whole body.'

Grey eyes glittered. 'I do know about your mother,' he said evenly. 'It was a great pity. Please accept my condolences.'

'Pity!' she screamed. 'You stand there and say it was a pity when it was one of your damned beloved horses that killed her!'

'You speak as though it was my fault,' he said tensely.

'It might well have been. You horse lovers are all the same. If you'd been there you'd probably have been more sorry that the horse had to be shot than because my mother was injured. And the fact that she never recovered helped put me off horses for life.

So if you can offer me no other job than mucking out your stables you're unlucky. I'll find myself a job elsewhere!'

Two bright spots of colour glowed in her cheeks and she was intensely conscious of the fact that he had been insolently eyeing her half-clad body as she spoke. She hugged the blanket in front of her.

'You do that,' he said quietly, but it was quite obvious that he was in a flaming temper, admirably controlled, but visible all the same. His grey eyes had darkened ominously and extra creases furrowed his brow. 'If you're able.'

Sherril thought he was referring to her limp and said defensively, 'Why shouldn't I? I'm perfectly capable.'

'I was not referring to your abilities,' he said tersely, 'but how you would transport yourself from here to wherever you chose to work. I don't think it's escaped your notice how isolated we are.'

'Too isolated,' flashed Sherril. 'But I could catch a bus.'

He shrugged. 'No buses run within five miles of here, the nearest town is twenty, according to your father you can't drive, and you refuse to go anywhere near a horse, so I can't see that you have any other alternative.'

She glared at him hostilely, unwilling to accede that he might be right. 'I'll find a way,' she said. 'It's ridiculous to accept that anyone in this day and age can be so cut off from civilisation.'

His eyes gleamed derisively. 'Only your own inadequacy makes you a prisoner. Why don't you forget your fears and take one of my horses? If you get out a bit more you might not be so bitter. Or does your leg stop you from riding too, like it does from learning to drive? Is that what's behind your unreasonable fear of horses?'

'It's not unreasonable,' snapped Sherril, angry with her father for discussing her with Nick Diamond. 'If you'd suffered how I have, you'd probably feel the same. I didn't spend months in a hospital for nothing.'

'Seems like they'd have done better repairing your tongue than your injured leg,' snarled the big man. 'What a great big chip you've got on your shoulder!'

He looked suddenly down at the lawn. 'Perhaps you ought to vent your temper out on that instead of me. Getting it mowed would do it far more good than lying on it.'

'Damn you!' snapped Sherril furiously. 'Do you think I would have been lying here if I had a mower? What do you expect me to do, cut it with a pair of scissors?'

'You have the time,' he said smoothly. 'Once you've done that, I'll see what else I can find you to do.'

With that he walked away and Sherril was left speechless, fuming inwardly, wishing she had something to throw at his retreating back.

CHAPTER TWO

IT took a long time for Sherril's temper to cool down. Even when her father returned several hours later she still had fire in her eyes.

Peter Martin took one look at her. 'What's wrong, Sherry love? You look as though you've been having a fight.'

'I have,' she rasped, 'with your boss. What a hateful man he is! How you can work for him I'll never know.'

He frowned. 'What have you been saying to Nick? I hope you haven't been rude to him again.'

Sherril turned on her father furiously. 'Why do you always blame me? It's him who's rude, he's the most detestable man I've ever had the misfortune to meet. I wish we'd never come here.'

He looked worried. 'I've never found Nick anything other than a gentleman. You must have said something to him, Sherry, if he was rude to you.'

'Oh, yes, I said something,' jeered Sherril. 'I told him I was going to get myself a job somewhere else. Why did you tell him why I wouldn't learn to drive? He took great delight in throwing it in my face.'

'You must have provoked him,' said her father. 'And why shouldn't I tell him? We were talking about you, he was interested.'

Sherril sniffed indelicately. 'I bet he was. Do you know what he's told me to do? Cut the lawn with a pair of scissors!'

To her annoyance her father burst out laughing. 'And you took him seriously? Oh, Sherry, you really are the limit!'

'Well, he didn't sound as though he was joking,' said Sherril huffily. 'He's taken as much a dislike to me as I have to him. I hate his guts, and I won't be responsible for my actions if we meet too often.'

Her father became suddenly serious. 'It's unlike you, my love, to dislike someone. You usually make friends easily.'

'Mr Diamond is different. He treats me as though I'm something the dog brought in. Do you really like him?'

Peter Martin nodded. 'Yes, Sherry, I do. He's a fine man, I've known him a long time, he's respected in the horse breeding world, trainers fall over themselves to buy his yearlings. I've never heard anyone have a bad word to say for him.'

'Except me,' she muttered. 'What have I done to deserve it?'

'I don't think he likes women much,' said her father, 'especially young precocious ones like you.' There was a twinkle in his eyes as he spoke. 'He's not married, that much I've found out. I believe someone let him down badly once, though no one's prepared to talk about it.'

'And he's venting his spite on me,' snapped Sherril. 'Why not Meg, or one of the other women? Why me?'

Her father shook his head. 'I don't think he's doing it deliberately, but you seem to have the knack of getting under his skin. Why don't you make an effort to be nice to him?'

'Why should I?' demanded Sherril, and then on a sudden worried note, 'It won't affect the way he treats you, will it, my arguing with him?'

A swift frown creased Peter Martin's brow, to be gone almost instantly, replaced with a fond smile for his daughter. 'Of course not.'

But she could see that he was worried and she promised herself that the next time she saw Nick Diamond she would try not to argue.

She had a nightmare that night. Nick Diamond was forcing her to cut a cricket pitch with a pair of nail scissors and every time she stopped he would lash out with a leather whip which he yielded with sadistic delight, his eyes gleaming like a devil.

She woke perspiring, hating the man even more, and wondering what she could do about the lawn at the back. Her dream had been so vivid that she had the feeling he might just come over today and make her cut it with a pair of scissors.

After breakfast she searched the garden shed for shears, but drew a blank, and wondered what old Bert used to keep it trimmed. Perhaps he had borrowed a mower from the house, their lawns were immaculate, or maybe Mr Diamond's gardener, or whoever did his lawns, had done Bert Jenkins' as well. He had been an old man, no one could have expected him to do it himself.

Yet Nick expected her to do it. With no implements. She could, of course, go up to his house and ask to borrow his mower, but she would die first.

Perhaps Jack Rowbotham had one? She would ask Meg when she came round for her now habitual cup of morning coffee. Talking to Meg was the highlight of Sherril's day. She would have laughed at the mere thought of it a few months ago. Her entertainment then had been derived from discos, parties and visits to the cinema.

What wouldn't she give now for a trip into Harrogate? A visit to the hairdressers, a meal out, an evening of entertainment. Such events were idle dreams these days.

When Meg arrived she took one look at Sherril's face and said, 'Now what's wrong? You look as though you have a load of worries.'

'Have you got a lawnmower?' asked Sherril bluntly, and had to laugh at the surprise on Meg's face.

'We have,' said Meg, 'but what's that got to do with it?'

'Orders,' replied Sherril. 'Orders from the big boss. He wants the lawn cutting.'

'And you haven't a mower. But that's not such a great problem, surely? Is that why you're looking so glum?' Meg filled the kettle when it became apparent that Sherril was not going to move from her chair. 'Or have you been arguing with him again?'

'Both,' admitted the younger girl. 'I don't think he likes to see anyone doing nothing. He caught me lying out there and said I ought to be cutting it instead.'

Meg smiled. 'But he wouldn't be serious. Nick's not like that.'

Sherril sank her head into her hands and said through gritted teeth, 'If anyone says that again I'll kick 'em! Nick's like that with me, whether you believe it or not. God knows what I've done, there's just something about me that he dislikes and he takes every opportunity to get at me. Can I borrow your mower?'

The other woman made the coffee and placed a cup before Sherril. 'Of course you can, we'll fetch it when we've finished this. I'll give you a hand.'

'You've done enough,' Sherril stirred sugar absently into her drink. 'Doesn't it drive you crazy living here day after day without ever going out? I think I'm slowly going nuts already.'

'You'll adapt,' replied Meg carefully. 'It's different, that's all, a different way of life. I wouldn't have it any other way.'

'But what do you do with yourself all day?' asked Sherril. 'You don't work for Nick too?'

Meg shook her head. 'But there's plenty to do. I bake and sew, and I love gardening, grow all my own vegetables and fruit. There's not enough hours in the day so far as I'm concerned.'

Such a picture of domesticity did not appeal to Sherril. Perhaps when she married and settled down she would change, but somehow she doubted it. She like people and parties, not animals and fresh air.

As soon as they had finished their coffee Meg led the way back to her cottage. But it was not until she opened the shed door that she clapped a hand on her mouth.

'Oh, Sherril, I've just remembered. It broke down, Jack's sent it away. It won't be back for another week. I am sorry. Why don't you ask Mr Diamond if you can borrow his, since he's the one who's complaining?'

'Not on your life,' said Sherril fervently. Her eyes alighted on a rusty frame at the back of the shed. 'Is that a bike? Can I borrow it?' An idea was already formulating in the back of her mind.

'Heavens!' exclaimed Meg. 'It's been there years. I doubt if it's any good. You can have it if you want, but I shouldn't think you'll get far on it.'

She moved several tins and boxes and a sack of fertiliser and between them they managed to lift the old bicycle clear. The tyres were flat and the pedals squealed complainingly, but it was all in one piece.

'Thanks,' said Sherril. 'I'll get this cleaned up in no time, and then I'm off. Who says I can't get a job in town? I'll show Mr Bighead Diamond a thing or two!'

Meg shook her head sadly. 'I hope you know what you're doing. I wouldn't like to trust myself on that contraption. Why don't you learn to drive if it's so important that you get away from here?'

'It will take too long,' said Sherril. 'Besides, who has time to teach me? No, this will do fine.'

She felt quite pleased with herself an hour or two later. She had oiled all the moving parts, wiped off as much of the rust and dirt as she could and blown up the tyres. The saddle didn't look too safe, so she tied it on with a piece of string, just in case, and then, forgetting all about the lawn, set off.

No one saw her go, for which she was thankful, as she wobbled along the narrow road. It had been many years since she rode a bicycle, and took more effort than she anticipated.

It was not as though the route was flat. The way out of the valley was uphill, and the road seemed endless, and by the time she had covered the five miles to the main road she was completely exhausted. Her legs felt ready to drop off and her tee-shirt stuck damply to her back, and she would have given anything for a drink.

She did not feel that she could go another mile, but she was determined now not to turn back, She rested for a while, sitting on the grass at the side of the road. One or two cars went by, but not many. They were well off the main route into Harrogate or York.

A quarter of an hour later Sherril mounted the cycle again. It was much more of an effort this time. Her legs did not seem to want to go, and the saddle had rubbed her sore, but she persevered, travelling mile after mile, glad that at least the road was level.

At a cross road she saw a sign pointing to Harrogate. It said twelve miles. She looked at her watch. Almost three—it shouldn't take her all that long to get there. She tried not to think about the journey back, or that she ought to have put off her trip until the next day and set out early in the morning.

It had somehow become imperative that she get away; she had felt that if she remained imprisoned in the valley a minute longer she would go mad.

She had travelled about three miles further when her feet went suddenly round and round on the pedals and nothing happened. Dismounting, she looked down and saw to her dismay that the chain had come off, and not only that, it had broken into three pieces.

Tears of frustration sprang to her eyes as she threw the vehicle down. 'Stupid damn bike!' she raged, taking a kick at it, at the same time knowing that it had been her own fault for attempting the journey on such an ancient contraption.

She sat down, resting her elbows on her knees, and her chin in her hands. 'What now?' she asked herself angrily. At a rough guess she had travelled twelve miles altogether, which meant that Harrogate was still eight miles away. But it was nearer!

Which was the lesser of the two evils, to walk into Harrogate and then hire a taxi or something to the Diamond stud, or attempt to walk back the way she had come?

It made sense to walk home, she could probably hitch a lift or perhaps even a bus might pass. A faint hope, she decided. She had not seen one all day.

She rested for an hour before summoning up the energy and determination. But she had walked for no more than a mile, pushing the fated bicycle, when she realised that it was going to be almost impossible.

Her limp became more pronounced with each step and every muscle ached from her unaccustomed exercise on the bike. It had been a stupid idea in the first place, she raged inwardly, sinking down again on the roadside, trying to fight back the tears of frustration and anger.

She glared at the endless hills on all sides of her, at the long ribbon of road. Unbidden came a quotation by J. B. Priestley that she had once read somewhere. 'In all my travels I've never seen a countryside to equal in beauty the Yorkshire Dales. The Dales have never disappointed me.'

Well, they had disappointed her. What was there but miles and miles of drystone walls, green hills with frequent outcrops of bare rock, running water, the odd farmhouse, clusters of trees and shrub.

Beautiful it might be, in certain people's eyes, but not to her, not right at this moment, when the most beautiful sight would have been a bus trundling towards her, or better still, her father in his car.

She set off again, stopping frequently, making slow progress, getting more and more angry as time went on. The fact that she could lay the blame on no one but herself did not help.

It took her about an hour to cover each mile. The odd car passed by, but no one took pity, they were too intent on speeding to wherever their destination lay to even notice the girl limping along the roadside.

Soon hunger added itself to her troubles and glancing frequently at her watch she saw the fingers creeping round hour by hour until it was well after nine.

Her father would be frantic. Why hadn't he come after her? Hadn't Meg told him what she had done?

Gradually it began to grow dark and she panicked in case she walked past the turning to Nick Diamond's place. Surely she must be getting close by now?

When she heard a vehicle approaching from behind, saw the beam of its lights cut into the dusk that surrounded her, she threw down the bike and stepped out. Now was no time to be cautious. She had had almost as much as she could take, her legs were not going to carry her much farther, and she did not relish the thought of spending the night sleeping under a hedge.

Waving her arms frantically, she stood in the middle of the road. The driver did not appear to see her at first, the vehicle's headlights bearing down frighteningly upon her. Her heart pounded and just as she was preparing to jump clear the driver slammed on his brakes, bringing the vehicle to a squealing halt.

She saw now that it was a Range Rover, but she wouldn't have cared had it been a tank. The driver jumped down and even before he reached her she could tell that he was angry, just by his actions.

'What the devil are you playing at? You could have got yourself killed!' And then as he saw who the girl was, 'Good God, it's you!'

Nick Diamond was the last man Sherril wanted to rescue her, but now was no time to be choosey. 'Yes, it's me,' she said flatly, and wished she did not feel like crying.

'What are you doing here—at this time of night—alone? God, anything could have happened to you.

Does your father know?'

Sherril shook her head, his angry words stimulating her, and forgetting her tears she cried, 'I'm not here from choice, if that's what you're thinking. My bicycle broke down, I——'

'Your—bicycle?' His loud guffaw echoed about them.

Enraged, she cried, 'I don't see what's so funny! Haven't you ever ridden a bike?'

He nodded, still laughing, 'Yes, but you—oh,' and he burst into more gales of laughter, 'you must have been desperate! Where did you get it, this beautiful vehicle that let you down when you least wanted it?'

Sherril glared haughtily. 'I don't see what it has to do with you. But since you ask, Meg gave it to me, Jack Rowbotham's wife.'

His brow shot up. 'Meg? I didn't know she had a bike. Where is it now, this famous steed of yours? Surely you've not left it on the roadside. What's the poor woman going to say?'

'I'm sorry I don't share your sense of humour,' said Sherril tightly, 'and I'm sorry I stopped you. If I'd known who it was I wouldn't have bothered.' She turned and began to walk away.

His hand clamped her shoulder and he spun her to face him. 'Aren't you being somewhat ridiculous?'

She glared hostilely. It was difficult to see his face with his back to the headlights, but she knew that the humour had gone and that he was now exceedingly angry.

But not as angry as she. He had made her feel a fool, and coming on top of her exhaustion she did not take it too kindly. 'I don't think so. You've made no secret of the fact that you don't like me, so why should I think you'd trouble yourself to give me a lift?'

'You imagine I'm hard-hearted enough to leave you stranded?' he snarled fiercely.

'Yes,' she snapped. 'Yes, I do, as a matter of fact.'

It was perhaps as well that she could not see his face, but his swiftly indrawn breath told her that she had not helped improve his temper. 'In that case,' he said harshly, 'I should hate you to be disillusioned.'

Swinging on his heel, he climbed back into the Range Rover. Sherril heard it crash into gear and soon there was nothing more to be seen than his red tail lights fast disappearing into the distance.

At first she could not believe that he had left her, but as the drone of the engine faded she was forced to face reality. She had accused him once of having no feelings, now she was convinced.

No man in his right mind would leave a defenceless woman out here at this time of night. Perhaps he was trying to teach her a lesson? Perhaps in a minute or two he would turn round and come back?

But as the seconds ticked by she knew that this was wishful thinking. Not that she would have accepted a lift, anyway, she told herself angrily. She wanted nothing from Nick Diamond, not ever.

Self-pity mingled with anger as she tramped slowly along. This time she left the bike behind. A rabbit scuttled out in front of her, frightening her, but probably she frightened the animal even more, because he turned back into the hedge in a desperate frenzy.

Twenty minutes elapsed and no vehicles passed her in either direction. An almost full moon illuminated her surroundings, much to her relief. The silence was eerie, the only sound her own footsteps dragging along the tarmac road.

Away in the distance the occasional light glimmered from an isolated farmouse. Of course she could go and ask for help, but a stubborn streak drove her on. If Nick Diamond wanted her to walk, then walk she would. No way would she give him the satisfaction of discovering that she had given in.

The road seemed endless, her steps got slower, the soles of her feet were so tender that it was agony to put one foot in front of the other.

When in the distance she saw headlights coming towards her she wondered for a moment whether her father's tough employer had had a change of heart, but as it drew nearer she realised that it was a car, and not the Range Rover.

But it was no use to her, going in the wrong direction, so with her head down she plodded on. When it stopped almost opposite she quickened her footsteps, all sorts of thoughts racing through her mind. One heard of such terrible happenings. Not that she stood much chance of escaping should it be anyone with an ulterior motive, she was so exhausted that she doubted whether she could manage another step.

'Sherry!'

Her father's voice broke into the darkness and

relief flooded over her, bringing with it a flood of
tears. She turned and fell into his arms. 'Oh, Daddy,
I'm so glad you've come!'

He murmured soothing words and led her to his
car, helping her inside and making sure she was
comfortable before resuming his own seat behind the
wheel.

Even then he did not start the engine straight
away. He slid his arm about her shoulders, pushing
his handkerchief into her hand. 'Suppose you tell me
what this is all about. I've been frantic with worry,
I had no idea where you'd gone.'

'D-didn't Meg tell you?' she sobbed. It had been
years since her father had taken her into his arms
like this, and she felt once again that she was the
little girl who had run to him with her troubles.

'I never thought of asking Meg,' he said, 'not until
it grew dark. That's when I really worried. When
she told me you'd gone off on her old bike I felt a bit
easier, but not much. I've been out looking for you,
but of course I didn't know which way you'd gone.'

She was already feeling better and smiled weakly.
'I'm sorry if I've been a nuisance, it's just that I was
so fed up, I felt that I had to get out somewhere or
I'd go mad.'

'I should have realised,' he said sadly. 'I ought to
have known that this was not the sort of life for a
young girl. We'll go back, Sherry, I can't have you
upsetting yourself like this. We'll go back to London,
we'll——'

'No, Daddy, no!' cried Sherril. 'It's not that bad.
You love your work here, I couldn't take you away.

I'll get used to it in time.'

'If you had something to do,' he said thoughtfully. 'You were all right while you were putting the cottage in order.'

'If you're going to suggest I take that job working for Mr Diamond, you can forget it,' she said vigorously. 'I'd rather die of boredom. I hate him!'

Peter Martin lovingly stroked the hair back from her face. 'Isn't hate rather a strong word? I'm sure he hasn't done anything to merit such a vehement reaction.'

Hasn't he? thought Sherril. You don't know half. 'Did he tell you he'd passed me and carried on without giving me a lift? I don't call that being a gentleman.'

Her father's shaggy brows rose. 'We met as I was coming out to search for you again. He said you were along this road and that he thought I ought to come and fetch you—he also said that you refused a lift from him.'

Sherril's head jerked up. 'I did no such thing!' She cast her mind back over their conversation. What was it she had said? That she thought him too hard-hearted to give her a lift, that had been it, and then he had gone. If he had told her father she had refused a lift then he had certainly twisted her words.

'That's what he intimated,' replied her father, and she knew that there was no point in trying to convince him otherwise. Nick Diamond was the cat's whiskers in her father's eyes, he thought the antagonism was all on her side.

'Let's go home,' she said tiredly. 'What wouldn't I give for a hot bath! I'm aching all over.'

Her father started the engine. 'It won't be long before you can do just that. I've fixed it up today, the builders are coming next week. They're going to build a bathroom on top of the kitchen extension. Apparently old Bert had the plans passed, but then he fell ill and never bothered.'

This was the best piece of news Sherril had heard since coming to the Diamond stud, and she smiled involuntarily. 'That's great, Daddy, that's wonderful. It will be almost like living in luxury.'

He patted her leg. 'That's my girl, you sound better already. By the way, what happened to the bike, I didn't see it?'

'It fell to pieces,' she grimaced, 'or at least the chain did. Perhaps you can fetch it tomorrow. I know it's not much good, but it does belong to Meg.'

'Besides which we can't leave it cluttering up the Yorkshire countryside,' said her father. 'It's so beautiful out here. I'm glad you didn't insist on returning to London,' adding quickly, 'though I would if it made you happy.'

'Darling Daddy!' Sherril leaned her head on his shoulder. 'You put up with it for Mummy's sake, I wouldn't dream of asking you to do it for me. Besides, I expect I shall get married in a year or two. I guess I can last out that long.'

Peter nodded happily. 'Once you get to know people you'll be fighting off the admirers, of that I'm sure. But I want you to promise me one thing, no more going off on your own—or at least tell someone. The last few hours have been some of the worst in my life. You don't know what thoughts were going through my head. I was on the verge of ringing the police.'

A few minutes later they were home. Never had the cottage seemed so welcoming. Her father filled a bowl with hot water and Sherril soaked her feet while sipping a mug of hot chocolate and devouring hungrily the cheese sandwiches he made her. They tasted good. The bread was new and thick and entirely different from the sliced bread she had been used to in the old house. It was delivered daily from a little bakehouse in Weirbrook and was one of the nicest things about this new life.

Sherril had discovered right from the first day that she had a splendid view of Nick Diamond's house from her bedroom window. Downstairs all that was visible were the chimneypots, her view restricted by the row of fir trees that bordered his garden.

But from this window her vantage point was perfect, and she looked out now, as she did most evenings before climbing into bed. She stiffened when she saw the master of the house standing on his front porch. He was easily seen by the light from the moon, leaning back nonchalantly against the ivy-clad stone.

Sherril knew that with the room behind in darkness she herself was invisible, but when he looked in her direction she shrank back, with the uneasy feeling that he knew she was there.

Had some sixth sense told him that he was being

watched? Or was it mere coincidence that he had chosen that precise moment to glance across at their cottage?

Was he wondering whether she was home yet, was his conscience perhaps pricking him that he had left her on the open road like that? She turned back the covers and climbed into bed. No way would that man's conscience bother him; it was doubtful he even had one.

Nevertheless she found it difficult to get to sleep. Nick Diamond was constantly on her mind, no matter how she tried to forget him. She was physically exhausted, yet her mind was over-active.

Was it only her he treated with such contempt? she wondered. Or was he the same towards his other employees? She had met only Jack Rowbotham and he had nothing but good to say for him, but how did the others feel?

Maybe it would help her get a better picture of this tough horse breeder if she ventured farther afield than their own little cottage and talked to some of them. Until now she had gone nowhere near the stables, or the fields where the horses were turned out during the daytime.

She knew why—she had been afraid of bumping into Nick Diamond and being forced into work she did not want to do. But looking at it in its proper perspective she realised that most probably he would not be about at all.

Her father was stud groom, he more or less ran the place. He had said himself that after the first few days Nick Diamond left him to it, had professed complete confidence in Peter's capabilities.

Tomorrow then, she decided, she would seek out some of the other men. She would not ask them directly what they thought of Nick, but maybe during the course of conversation a general picture would emerge.

Exactly why she was so interested in this man she could not say, except that she had never met anyone like him before and was curious as to what made him tick.

Once her mind was relaxed Sherril slept, not waking until her father brought a cup of tea to her room. 'You're spoiling me,' she protested, accepting it gladly all the same.

'If I can't spoil my own daughter it's a pity,' he smiled. 'I thought you might like a lie in after your adventure yesterday. How are you feeling?'

Sherril flexed her limbs experimentally. 'A bit stiff, but not too bad, I don't think. I thought I might get you to introduce me to some of the stud hands, it's about time I got to know them.'

A smile of relief lightened her father's face, made him look younger. He had aged, she thought, since her mother died, looked older than his forty-nine years. His hair which, until then had retained its natural brown colour, had grown almost white, but for a few seconds as she spoke he had looked his old self, and she realised that his happiness was in her own hands. He was concerned for her, she was the only family he had left, and if she was unhappy then he was too.

He nodded. 'I'll come back for you later, give you

time to get washed and eat your breakfast. I'm glad
you're beginning to take an interest, I was getting
quite concerned.'

When he had gone Sherril finished her tea, but
when she put her feet to the floor drew them back
again quickly. It hurt! On inspection she discovered
that the blisters had burst, probably rubbed by the
sheets as she slept.

Gingerly she made her way downstairs to the first
aid box which they kept in the kitchen and pressed
sticking plaster over all the sore spots. After that she
washed and dressed and had just finished a slice of
toast when her father returned.

'Ready?' He appraised his daughter in her crisp
white cotton blouse and brown corduroy pants. 'The
men are sure going to love you. You're the prettiest
person on the farm, and I'm proud of you.'

Sherril glowed and walked with her father down
the lane and through the gates leading into the
Diamond stud. They approached the long neat rows
of looseboxes, each in immaculate order.

Popping her head over one of the doors, Sherril
noted the thick straw bedding, the plentiful supply
of cold water. There was not a thing out of place,
and it made her all the more raw when she recalled
the condition of their own cottage. Apparently Nick
Diamond thought more of his horses than he did his
employees.

In the last stable a lad of no more than eighteen
had just finished cleaning out the soiled straw. 'Jim,
this is my daughter, Sherril. Jim's the youngest
hand,' he explained as the grinning boy eyed Sherril

unashamedly. 'Gets easily distracted,' he continued in soft reprimand.

The lad looked away quickly and Sherril and her father moved on. 'You'll get plenty of that if you continue to wear those tight trousers,' said Peter Martin, but he was not complaining.

Another man was sweeping the yard. 'Hello, Sam,' said her father. 'This is my daughter, she's come to have a look around.'

Sam held out his hand. 'Pleased to make your acquaintance, miss. Going to work here, are you? We could certainly do with a bit of glamour about t' place.'

Sam was in his thirties, a fine-looking man with a ruddy complexion and a twinkle in his blue eyes.

Peter said immediately, 'Sherril's unfortunately a bit timid where horses are concerned. She got thrown badly as a child, never got over it.'

'You will, living here,' said Sam confidently. 'Go and see t' foals, if they don't get through to you no one will.'

Sherril liked Sam, there was something about him that appealed. Maybe here was the man who could tell her about Nick Diamond.

When her father led her away she called over her shoulder, 'I'll see you around sometime, Sam,' and he winked. Yet she knew he meant nothing by it. He was a safe sort of man, a solid earthy type, a sort she had not met when they lived further south.

Pointing out the harness room and storehouse, and the big barn which housed the hay, her father led her past the foaling block, which was clinically clean

and had heating as well as lighting and a really thick
bed of straw.

The whole was kept in immaculate order with not
a piece of loose straw blowing about anywhere. All
the men to whom she was introduced were busily at
work on their respective jobs, but all had a minute
to spare to admire the new stud groom's daughter.

After their tour her father said, 'Shall we go and
see the horses now? Like Sam said, the foals are a
picture, you can't help loving them. Nick has twelve
mares and all but one foaled in March. He thought
Pasadena Lady was barren, but apparently not, she
expects her foal in about a month. That's something
I'm really looking forward to.'

'I think we'll leave them for now,' said Sherril, 'I
ought to be getting your lunch.'

He glanced at his watch. 'It's too soon for that,
but if you don't want to, I won't force you. Perhaps
some other time?'

She nodded. 'Yes, Dad, some other time.'

She knew she had to face them, that sooner or
later she would have to get over her phobia, but she
wasn't ready for it, not yet. She had surprised herself
by going as far as the stables, it was something she
would not have done a few months ago. When her
mother died she swore that she would never have
anything to do with horses again, and she wouldn't
have done, had it not been for her father's job.

She was surprised it hadn't turned him off them,
but he showed not the slightest sign of bitterness or
rancour. He said the horse involved could not be
blamed, that he had got scared when the horsebox

that had been transporting him had been involved in the accident, kicking his way out and careering wildly along the street, ears back and teeth bared. It was unfortunate her mother happened to be one of the victims hit by his flying hooves.

The blow, in her stomach, had caused internal damage and despite several operations she had unfortunately never pulled through.

No, Sherril felt she could not bear to go and gaze at the mares in the paddocks. The memories they would certainly evoke would be all too painful.

She left her father and returned to the cottage, going straight into the kitchen and filling the kettle. To her amazement Nick Diamond was standing in the centre of the lawn—and it had been cut!

But it was not this fact that concerned her now, but that he had the cheek to come on to their property. She did not stop to think that the cottage belonged to him. They lived in it and so far as she was concerned it was theirs, and he had no right being here.

At the same time as she saw him he looked across and coming round to the side door which led directly into the kitchen he pushed it open and walked inside.

That he had entered without even knocking enraged her even more. She said distantly, 'What do you want, Mr Diamond?'

The hard grey eyes were unflinching. 'You've mowed the lawn, I see. Good. That should mean that you have nothing to do and as one of my lads is going on holiday at the weekend you can take over his duties until he returns.'

'No, thank you,' she returned. 'I've told you before that mucking out doesn't appeal in the slightest.'

His eyes narrowed. 'The way I see it you have no choice, Miss Martin. Your father promised you would help out, let's say it was a condition of his getting the job.'

'My father knows how I feel about horses,' she flashed. 'I'm quite sure he would promise nothing so rash.'

'Ask him,' shrugged the big man, hooking a chair towards him with one foot and straddling it backwards. 'Are you making tea? I could do with a cup.'

He dominated the tiny room. One would have to be blind not to be aware of his physical attributes, and Sherril was aware of a slight quickening of her pulses when he looked at her. She wanted to scream at him to get out, to yell that in no way would she ever give him a cup of tea, unless it had arsenic in it. But he was her father's employer, and unless she wanted to jeopardise his job she supposed she had better give at least an outward show of politeness. No matter that inside she was seething.

Her mouth was grim as she busied herself setting out cups, and she stood resolutely with her back to him as she waited for the water to boil, staring out of the window, wondering who the good Samaritan was who had mown their lawn for them.

But the time came when she had to face him, and she discovered that he had been watching her, an enigmatic expression in his grey eyes, and it disconcerted her, so that her hand trembled as she filled the pot, water spilling over on to the table.

She felt his disapproval, though he said nothing, and this made her worse, so that when she began to pour their teas he took the pot from her. 'What a state you're in! Are you normally like this?'

'No, I'm not,' she snapped, before she could stop herself.

'Then it must be me,' he said. 'Perhaps I ought to apologise, though I'm sure I don't know what I've done.'

Sherril glared. 'Simply being here is enough. Please hurry and finish your tea. I have my father's lunch to prepare.'

'Just as soon as you promise you'll come and work for me,' he said, eyeing her over the rim of his cup.

'But that's blackmail!'

He shrugged. 'So what? I'm shorthanded, you have nothing to do. It's an ideal solution. Of course, if you want to see your father out of work, and at his age it won't be easy to find another job, then that's your problem.'

'Damn you!' she cried. 'Is this how you employ all your labour? For such an esteemed character I can't say I think much of your tactics.'

'And I don't think a lot of your manners,' he said coldly, finishing his tea and standing up. 'I shall expect you to report for duty at half past seven on Saturday morning. If you don't—well, I think you know what the consequences will be.'

CHAPTER THREE

THE moment Sherril's father came in for lunch she cried heatedly, 'He's done it again, that man you all so reverently look up to! He's insisted that I work for him while one of his lads is on holiday.'

'Young Jim,' nodded Peter Martin. 'I was wondering how we'd manage without him. He makes a good job of those stables, and doesn't grumble either, not like a lot of the youngsters these days.'

'Do you realise what I said?' insisted Sherril, shaking her father's shoulder. 'He wants me to do Jim's job!'

Her father looked at her steadily. 'I know.'

'And you don't object?'

'You'd have help. I think it's about time you did something, Sherril. You'd have less time to feel bored and——'

'I might have known you'd be on his side,' she cut in angrily. 'I wouldn't be surprised if you weren't in collusion. I'm a secretary, you know, not a skivvy!'

'But, love,' said her father anxiously, 'there are no secretarial jobs near here. If you could drive you could take my car. You have no choice really.'

Sherril glared. 'Are you afraid he'll carry out his threat if I don't? Personally I don't believe him, I think he's trying it on simply to get me working.'

'Threat?' frowned Peter Martin. 'I don't know what you're talking about. Nick wouldn't blackmail you into working for him, I'm quite sure of that.'

'Then you'd better ask him,' snapped Sherril. 'He said that if I didn't you'd be out of a job.'

He laughed but looked worried all the same. 'Nonsense, Sherry. I can't believe that of Nick. He was having you on.'

She shrugged. 'It's what the man said, and I for one think he's hard-hearted enough to do it. For some reason he's taken an instant dislike to me.'

'You're imagining it,' said her father, 'Let's forget the whole subject. Is supper ready? I'm starving!'

Unappeased, Sherril slammed his meal down in front of him. She had intended making a steak and kidney pie, her father's favourite, but after Nick Diamond's visit she felt like kicking the hell out of everything in sight and had done nothing more than grill chops and tomatoes.

'I'm going out,' she said, 'I'm not hungry,' and before her father could stop her she had gone. She made her way over to Meg's house, feeling the need to talk to someone of her own sex.

The other woman was delighted to see her. 'I've been hearing about your escapade on the bike,' she said, welcoming her inside. 'I came over this morning, but you were out. Sit down and tell me all about it.'

'There's nothing to tell,' shrugged Sherril, sinking into a cretonne-covered chair in Meg's comfortable sitting room. 'It let me down and I had to walk.'

'I'm not surprised,' said Meg. 'I hear you were going to Harrogate. What possessed you to try and get that far? I had no idea. I could have told you you'd never make it, not on that old boneshaker.'

Sherril smiled ruefully. 'I've not really come to discuss that. Where's Jack, is he out?'

'Taking a shower,' replied Meg. 'He'll be ages yet. What is it, girl talk?'

'Nick Diamond talk,' said Sherril heatedly. 'He wants me to help muck out the stables.'

Meg wrinkled her nose. 'Not my idea of fun, but it's a job that has to be done, and I'm sure he'll pay you a fair wage. At least that's one advantage.' She grinned impishly. 'You can save up for a new bike.'

'Not likely,' scoffed Sherril. 'And I suppose it's not so much the work, though I don't fancy it very much, but the fact that he gave me an ultimatum. He said that if I didn't do it my father would lose his job. Daddy doesn't believe me, he thinks he was only joking, but he wasn't, Meg, honestly.'

Meg shook her head. 'I'm afraid I don't believe it either.' She looked apologetic. 'Nick Diamond's not like that. Ask Jack, ask any of the men.'

'Well, let me put it this way,' insisted Sherril irately. 'I shall go and do that job, even though I'm dead set against it, simply because I don't want my father out of work. If I thought he was joking, do you think I'd give in?'

Meg shook her head slowly. 'Knowing you, Sherril, no. You've already shown me what a hot temper you have and I know that you never let anyone put on you. Perhaps you misinterpreted him, that's all.'

'You think I shouldn't turn up on Saturday? You

think I ought to call his bluff?'

'We—ell . . .' The other woman looked dubious.

'You see?' pounced Sherril. 'You're not sure. No, he was serious all right. Why he hates my guts I've no idea, but the feeling's mutual, you can rest assured on that. He's the most despicable man I've ever had the misfortune to meet!'

Jack came in and caught the tail end of her sentence. 'Who are we discussing? You sound positively venomous!'

'I am,' gritted Sherril, 'and it's your dear boss.'

'Oh!' he mouthed. 'Say no more. I'm well aware that there's no love lost between you.' Then he grinned suddenly. 'But you know what they say about hate?'

'Like hell,' declared Sherril loudly. 'I'd never love that man, not in a thousand years. I wish Daddy had never come here, I really do. But'—she squared her shoulders—'I shan't let him down.' She stood up. 'Thanks for listening, Meg, I'll go and see if Daddy's finished his supper.'

'I'm sorry I couldn't be any help,' said Meg, 'but I think in all fairness we can say that we know Nick Diamond better than you.'

Sherril nodded. They knew one side of him, yes, but not the side he presented to her. It was maddening that everyone thought she was lying, but there was not a lot she could do about it unless some irrefutable evidence came up to convince them, and she could not see that that was ever likely to happen.

Peter Martin had finished his meal and was outside staring at the newly mown lawn. 'Did he say anything about this?' he wanted to know.

'He commented on the fact that it was cut,' she admitted. 'Who did it? I was absolutely amazed.'

'I borrowed Sam's mower,' he said. 'And I've ordered a new one. We shouldn't have any problems in future.' He smiled weakly, as though unsure of his daughter's mood. 'I couldn't have you down on your hands and knees with a pair of scissors, could I?'

She shook her head crossly. 'You think I'm making all this up, but I'm not. You'll see in the end.'

The next day Sherril spent lazing about the house, chatting to Meg when she came across for her morning coffee, studiously avoiding any mention of Nick Diamond.

She went to bed early and got up at seven with her father. He too was careful to make no mention of his employer, going out of the house before Sherril. 'We have to move the horses into the paddocks,' he explained. 'If you want to come and help you're welcome,' but he knew she would refuse.

'No, thanks,' she said tightly. 'I'll be across shortly.' She wore jeans and a thin sweater, for the morning air was cool, but she had no boots or wellingtons so had to make do with a pair of flat walking shoes.

The yard was deserted and she looked into the first stable, wrinkling her nose at the unaccustomed smell. Her father always said that the smell of horses was the best smell in the world, but she could not agree.

She stood there wondering what to do, when Sam approached. He grinned. 'Come to help? You're a far prettier sight than Jim. I might enjoy mucking out with you to feast my eyes on. Done this sort of thing before? No! I'm surprised, with your father so keen on horses.'

'I'm afraid the feeling's not mutual,' said Sherril. 'Besides me being thrown Mummy was killed by a runaway horse. It's put me off them for life.'

'I see,' he said thoughtfully. 'But it's a start, helping in t'stables. Very plucky. Who knows, we might even get you back on a horse before long.'

He was sympathetic and interested and Sherril had not the heart to disagree. She nodded and smiled and said, 'Shall we begin?'

He showed her how to fork out the soiled straw, and where to empty the barrow, where the fresh straw was kept, and where the water supply was. 'It's hard work, mind, if you're not used to it.'

He could not have spoken a truer word, thought Sherril two hours later. It took her an hour to do each stable, and each forkful of manure seemed heavier than the last so that her actions became progressively slower.

At this rate, she thought, I shall be here all day. There were nearly thirty stables in all. She wondered how many she was expected to do and found it impossible to accept that Jim did them all on his own.

Soon her hands began to blister and with hindsight she wished she had worn gloves. But she was determined not to admit defeat. It was what Nick Diamond would love.

She was surprised that he had not come to see how she was doing, but guessed it would not be long before he did. The thought was sufficient to keep her at it, although by now it was so painful to wield the fork that she almost felt like crying.

Her back ached, her shoes were thickly coated in manure, as were the bottoms of her jeans, and the worst part about it was that she could not even have a bath. She would have to encroach on Meg's generosity again and use her shower.

At lunchtime her father came to look for her, exclaiming in concern over her bleeding hands. 'My dear child, why haven't you put something on them? You can't carry on like that!'

'Try telling Nick Diamond,' she snapped, gladly putting down her fork and accompanying her father back to their cottage.

She kicked off her shoes outside, looking ruefully down at her jeans, rolling up the bottoms so that at least the muck was hidden. There was no point in changing, she thought. There was several more hours' work to be got through yet.

After washing her hands, and carefully patting them dry, she sat on one of the kitchen chairs while her father cut sandwiches and made a pot of tea. 'The trouble with you is that you're not used to hard work.' But he smiled as he spoke and Sherril accepted it with a sad smile.

'Can you do anything with these?' she asked, holding up her hands. The raw spots were bleeding again and she realised fatalistically that if she had to do this work for a whole week they would never get a chance to heal.

Damn Nick Diamond! How she wished she had never heard the sound of his name.

Tutting in concern, her father cleansed her hands

tenderly with cotton wool, dabbing on antiseptic and then sticking plasters over each of the raw blisters. 'You'd better put gloves on this afternoon,' he said. 'I ought to have warned you that mucking out is not kind to delicate hands. Still, after a few days you'll feel you've been at it all your life.'

'If it doesn't kill me first,' she said bitterly. 'My back feels as though it's breaking.'

'You'll get used to it,' he said, and it looked as though that was all the sympathy she was going to get from him. Having been used to this sort of work all his life he could not understand why his daughter found it so hard.

When it was time to return Sherril lifted herself from the chair with difficulty, forcing her aching limbs to move, wondering how she was going to get through the rest of the day without collapsing.

Sam was already at work and she noticed to her relief that there were only a couple more stables to do. He certainly got through them at a far greater speed than herself.

Even wearing gloves she found the pain in her hands almost more than she could bear and was profoundly thankful when they had finished.

'Only t' yard to be swept now,' said Sam, handing her a brush.

Sherril looked in horror at the vast amount of yard, at the wisps of straw and muck that had inevitably blown across it as they worked. 'Do we have to?' she asked wearily. 'What are the others doing, why can't they help?'

'They'll be schooling the foals,' he said. 'That's

something you ought to watch, it can be quite entertaining.'

'Opportunity would be a fine thing,' said Sherril irritably, but she knew that she wouldn't, even if she had the time. Working so close to horses was making her no fonder of them.

Once the yard was clean, with not one scrap of straw to mar its perfection, she heaved a sigh of relief. That was it for today at least. All she felt like now was a good wash and a rest, but when she returned to her cottage she found to her intense annoyance that Nick Diamond was waiting for her.

She bit back a heated question, instead merely raising her fine brows. For a few long seconds they stared at each other, Sherril vitally aware of his physical charms, of his clean male freshness. He made her feel like a tramp, and she knew she did not smell very sweet.

'You look as though your first day's work has exhausted you,' he said, looking her up and down, noting her bent back and her filthy shoes, her hands with their sticking plaster which was by now soaked in blood.

'Oh, it was nothing,' she said airily. 'I always look like this after I've been working.' She pushed open the cottage door. 'If you want to see me about something you'd best come inside.'

His disturbing presence made her forget her shoes, and it was not until she saw him looking down that she realised she had trodden manure into her kitchen.

'Damn!' she exclaimed furiously, pulling them off and throwing them outside.

'Surely you haven't worked in those?' Nick

Diamond looked incredulous.

'I had no alternative,' she replied distantly. 'I don't possess any wellingtons.'

'You could have borrowed some. There are several pairs in the house from which you can take your pick.'

'And how was I supposed to know, since no one bothered to tell me?' she demanded angrily. 'If you'll excuse me, I'll slip upstairs and change my jeans.'

Why he had come she did not know, unless it was to gloat. Perhaps he had thought she would not even finish the job, that it would be too much for her. He did not know her well enough to realise that she would never let a man like him get the better of her.

When she came back down he had put on the kettle and set out two cups and saucers. But far from being pleased she was extremely annoyed. 'You're making yourself very much at home, aren't you? If you don't mind, this is my cottage, I prefer to work in it myself.'

'I thought you looked tired,' he said.

'You know damn well I'm tired,' she flashed back, 'but that's no excuse. You have no right forcing your way in here!'

'Correction. You invited me,' he said, and there was a warning glint in his grey eyes that sent a shudder through her. 'And from the look of those hands you're not capable of doing much. Would you like me to renew your plasters?'

'Like hell I would! My father will do them when he comes home.'

'Since that will be several hours I suggest you stop being childish and let me do it.'

Before she could protest he had lifted one of her hands and though she pulled back he held her wrist in a vice-like grip.

Not wishing to lose her dignity by struggling, Sherril allowed him to peel off the soiled plasters. His tenderness surprised her, she had imagined he would rip them off, even take great delight in doing so.

He exclaimed when he saw how raw her hands were.

'What did you expect?' she snapped. 'I'm no stable girl, I'm not used to hard work—no—that's not right, I'm not used to manual work.'

She had never been this close to Nick Diamond before, and was disconcerted to discover that her heart beats had increased. Fervently she willed him to hurry, but as though aware of her feelings he leisurely bathed her wounds, patting them dry and smoothing on an antiseptic cream before fixing new plasters.

'What sort of work did you do before you came here?' he enquired indolently. 'Or were you a lady of leisure, enjoying one round of social parties after another.'

She tossed her head scornfully. 'Is that the picture you get of me?'

'I think you're spoilt,' he said. 'Your father lets you get away with too much.'

'Thank you,' snapped Sherril, snatching her hand free the moment he had finished and backing away.

'When I want your opinion I'll ask for it!'

He held out his hand. 'The other one, please.'

She gritted her teeth and reluctantly allowed him to take it, deciding that the more she saw of Nick Diamond the less she liked him. He was insufferably rude as well as all the other things she could call him. It amazed her how he could tend to her abrasions so gently, she would not have thought he had a gentle streak in him.

'As a matter of fact,' she said, 'I was a secretary, and a jolly good one too. My employer was very disappointed to see me go and said it was doubtful he would find anyone else to come up to my standards.'

'I'm pleased to hear you're good at something,' he replied caustically. 'I'd begun to wonder. I mean, you can't or won't ride a horse, you can't drive a car, you can't ride a bicycle without getting into difficulties, you can't mow a lawn, mucking out stables is too much for you, judging by the state of your hands. The list is endless—would you like me to go on?'

'I'd like you to get out of here,' snapped Sherril, her face flaming, green eyes flashing. 'You're the most insolent man I've ever met! What I've done to deserve this, I've no idea, but I certainly don't intend taking much more!'

He smiled mockingly. 'And what will you do about it? Your working today proves you're scared your father will lose his job if you do defy me. I have you where I want you, Miss Sherril Martin, and strange as it may seem I'm rather enjoying it.'

'I've no doubt about that,' she spat tightly. 'You're making it perfectly clear.'

The second he had finished she moved away, glaring hostilely. 'Will you go now, please? I've had about as much of you as I can stand for one day.'

'You don't know why I came,' he said calmly. 'Aren't you interested?'

'Not in the least.' The fact that he had the power to disturb her made her all the more angry. Her pulses had raced like crazy while he had been near and all she wanted now was for him to leave.

He was sexually exciting, something she had not realised before, and because she hated him it made her even angrier that she had unwittingly been made aware of his fatal charm.

'I thought you'd like to know that the builders can get here earlier than promised,' he continued. 'They're coming on Monday. It shouldn't be long before you'll be able to indulge yourself fully.'

'Everyone bathes,' snapped Sherril heatedly. 'You seem to be insinuating that I'm the only person who's complaining. I bet you have a bathroom, and I bet you use it every day.'

'But of course,' he grinned. 'Not that I object to the smell of horses, there's something rather satisfying about it.'

'Or you get so used to it that you don't notice. But I do, and I think it's foul, and as I can't wait until the bathroom's built I'm going round to Meg Rowbotham's right now to use her shower.'

He smiled, a somewhat satisfied smile, she thought, and the next moment knew why. 'She's out.

Jack's gone into York for me, and Meg's gone with him.'

'Oh, damn!' If she hadn't been working she could have gone too, got that curtain material they needed, and a few personal items that she was getting desperate for.

Thick brows rose. 'I don't approve of ladies swearing.'

'I'm no lady,' she yelled, 'at least not in your presence. If it hadn't been for your damn—your insistence that I muck out the stables I could have gone too. There are several things I need.'

'A pity you never took your father up on his offer of driving lessons. I imagine you're regretting it now.'

'I'm regretting a lot of things,' she flung viciously, 'and one of them is meeting you!'

A frown darkened his handsome face. 'It may come as no surprise that I too am almost beginning to regret setting on your father. I've known Peter a long time, he's mentioned you often, but quite obviously his parental love blinds him to your faults.'

'Daddy never mentioned you,' she said strongly. 'I'd——'

'Quite obviously,' he broke in. 'You wouldn't have come here if you'd known about me. Isn't that what you were about to say? Another of your little traits, Miss Martin. You're as easy to read as the open pages of a book.'

She tossed her head scornfully and refused to answer.

'I think it's time for that cup of tea,' he said, 'Shall

I make it or will you?'

Since she could not see him going until he had
had his drink Sherril gave in with ill grace. 'I will.'
She reboiled the kettle and poured water into the
pot to warm it, aware that he was watching her every
move.

The silence was almost worse than when they were
arguing, unnerving her, and his cup rattled in it
saucer as she handed it to him.

'I don't see why you couldn't have told my father
about the builders,' she said, feeling the need to say
something.

'I thought you were the one who was more interested in the bathroom.' Nick's eyes twinkled and she
knew he mocked.

'Personal hygiene is of importance to both my
father and me,' she said. 'It's no fun washing down
at the kitchen sink, you ought to try it some time.'

'I've had my share of roughing it,' he said, but
she did not believe him. She knew that the stud had
been handed down by his father, so in what way
had he suffered hardship?.

'Really?' she said, her green eyes scornful.

'Really,' he jeered, 'and since I can see you don'
believe me, I'll tell you. As soon as my schooling
was finished my father turned me out into the world
without a penny to my name. He hadn't got to where
he was without sheer hard work, he told me. If I
proved I could make it on my own, then the stud
would be mine, otherwise it would be sold.'

'He sounds cruel,' remarked Sherril.

'A hard man,' he admitted, 'but fair. He realised

hat I would never appreciate the true value of
money if it was always there for the asking.'

'Did he love you?' asked Sherril, knowing that her
father would never boot her out like that.

Nick Diamond nodded. 'Very much. He told me
later that it was the hardest thing he'd ever done,
but he never had any regrets, I'm glad to say.'

'You obviously made good,' she said sarcastically.
'What did you do?'

For a moment she thought he was not going to
tell her, and then as though deciding that he might
as well go through with it since he had started, he
said, 'I got myself a job as a stable hand to begin
with, at Newmarket, near your part of the world.'

Sherril wondered what she would have thought of
him if they had met then, but realised that it must
be all of fifteen years ago, and she would have been
but a child.

'It was my burning ambition to be a jockey,' he
continued, 'but as you can see,' grimacing ruefully,
'I grew rather too much. Horses were in my blood,
though, and I could see no other life, so I saved as
much of my wages as I could and I bought a filly.

'In every second of my spare time I trained her.
Black Diamond I called her, her coat was like silk,
her muscles rippled as she moved, her mane and tail
flew proudly. I can see her now.'

There was a gleam in his eyes that Sherril had
never seen before; his mind was far away, reliving
those days when he was a youth. Quite obviously
Black Diamond had been the love of his life.

'When she was ready I managed to find someone

to ride her and I entered her for a race, and despite the gloomy forecasts from everyone in the racing fraternity, she won. I knew she would, she was a magnificent horse.'

'And what happened?' Sherril was interested despite herself.

His face suddenly became sad. 'I was offered a handsome sum for her, far more than I could ever have made out of racing, so I sold her.'

'Oh!' There seemed nothing else to say.

He shrugged. 'That's business. I bought two more yearlings and very soon I'd made a good profit on them too. I was on my way up.'

'Did you mind giving up training to become a breeder?'

'It never occurred to me that I would ever be anything else,' he said. 'It was what my father wanted. Training horses was merely a step in the right direction. The old man was proud of me. In fact we've a couple of mares here now whose dam was Black Diamond, so you see, I still have something to remind me of her. Would you like to see them?'

Sherril immediately retreated into her shell, freezing up inside. It was not something she could help, her fear of horses was so great that she knew it would be with her all her life. 'No!' she said abruptly, then 'I'm sorry, but I can't help how I feel.'

'You could help yourself,' he said gently.

She shot him a startled glance, her green eyes wide. He sounded almost human, and this was certainly not the mental picture she had of him. 'You don't understand,' she protested. 'You love horses, therefore you can see no reason why everyone else doesn't.'

'I can see no reason why you let two incidents prejudice you for life,' he said tersely. 'If anyone has a reason to hate horses, it's your father. Yet his love of them has in no way diminished.'

She shrugged and remained silent.

'The horse didn't kick your mother deliberately. He was frightened, in fact I reckon he was close to panic. You'd react in exactly the same way if you found yourself in an unnatural situation, scared out of your wits.'

Sherril could not deny his logic, but it did not help matters. Her fear, fast developing into a phobia, was very real in her own mind, and nothing that anyone said could make any difference.

'Most probably,' she agreed, 'but you forget that I already had a good reason for hating horses, my mother's accident merely deepened my feelings.'

'Oh, yes, the fall, hence the limp—a perpetual reminder, or so you probably keep telling yourself.'

His goading words drew a quick flash of anger. 'My leg was broken in two places, and one of the fractures had to be set again because of complications. It was no fun, I can tell you.'

'You have my every sympathy.' The grey eyes regarded her coolly.

'Don't be funny,' she snapped. She had almost forgotten her hatred when he was talking about himself. It proved that there was a compassionate side to his nature, a side which everyone else saw but rarely she herself. But now all her old fury returned. 'I know you think I've been stupid to let it affect me so much, but——'

'I don't think,' he cut in brusquely. 'I know. But all you've succeeded in doing is ruining your own life. You'd be a free agent now if you'd forgotten your leg and learned to drive. I appreciate the mental torture you're suffering penned in this place, and begrudgingly I'll admit that you did a fine thing coming here with your father. He did need you, he also needed this job, it's helping him come to terms with himself.'

Sherril replaced her empty cup into its saucer. 'Big deal, Mr Diamond. Thank you very much for those few kind words, they've made my day.'

Nick frowned at her raw sarcasm, 'Typical,' he grated. 'I might have known you wouldn't know how to accept a compliment.'

'A backhanded compliment is no good to anyone.' She pushed herself up from the table. 'Haven't you any work to do, Mr Diamond? You boast so glibly of the way you proved your worth, but I can't say I've ever seen you doing anything. Is it fun to hold the whip hand, have everyone else running around for you?'

He was violently angry now, his eyes glinted dangerously and his lips were drawn into a grim line He too rose and held himself proudly above her, towering like a giant, drawing in his breath and saying harshly, 'Don't push me too far, Miss Martin, or there'll be another episode in your life that you may later live to regret.'

She tilted her chin, her honey-blonde hair quivering as she strove to keep a rein on her temper. 'It sounds like I've hit on the truth,' she said tightly.

Their eyes met and held until he swung away in disgust. 'You think what you want, young lady, just bear in mind that you're not doing yourself any good by continually crossing me.'

'I don't see that it makes any difference either way,' she retorted. 'You hate my guts and I hate yours, it's as simple as that. So far as I'm concerned the best thing would be for us to keep out of each other's way—permanently.'

'You'd like that, wouldn't you?' He faced her again and there was something on his face that made her breath catch in her throat. 'But I'm not going to give you that pleasure. I'm almost beginning to enjoy these little—meetings of ours, except when you go too far, then I feel like putting my hands round your slender throat and——'

'I should have known your were a sadist as well,' she flashed. 'Go on, then, if it will give you pleasure,' and she boldly pushed her body against his, tilting her chin, holding her hair up from the back of her head with her hands.

His breath deepened. 'I'm sorely tempted, Sherril Martin, but if you continue to press your delectable body against mine for much longer, there are other things I shall do.'

She flushed, getting his meaning, but perversely decided to call his bluff. 'I don't think so, Mr Diamond. You'd have my father to account to if you did.'

'I'd tell him you threw yourself at me,' he said, a peculiar glint in his eyes. 'He'd believe me—and of course it's true, you couldn't deny that.'

Deliberately he lowered his eyes, looking at her breasts, high and proud, even more pronounced by the position of her arms. 'Beautiful,' he said, 'and being offered to me freely.'

Before she had time to realise what he was doing he was touching them, stroking, gently teasing, an action that sent fire coursing through her veins, and the next moment his mouth was on hers, fiercely possessing, not stopping until the blood pounded in her head and she was gasping for breath. Even then he allowed her only a few seconds' respite before he was hungrily kissing her again, forcing her lips back against her teeth.

Fire coursed through her veins, an unwitting response, which she savagely tried to ignore. With a cry of fury she pummelled her hands on his chest, 'Just what do you think you're doing? Take your hands off me this instant!'

'You told me to give myself pleasure,' he said in mock indignation.'

'Not in that way,' she grated. 'Trust you to twist my words round—I've noticed that you're pretty expert at that sort of thing.'

'I'm expert at many things,' Nick said blandly, 'You've made your hand bleed again.'

She had been so incensed that she had not felt the hurt, but now she realised just what she had done. Blood oozed from the edges of two of the plasters, there were spots on his shirt, and her hands felt more sore than before.

'And I used the last plaster,' he said, with a pretence of apology. 'I've a good supply up at the house. Come with me and I'll give you some. Oh, and while you're there, you may as well use my bathroom. I think I agree, you do smell rather pungent.'

'It's your manure off your rotten horses,' cried Sherril indignantly. He needn't have rubbed it in quite so blatantly—amazingly she had become accustomed to the smell herself. 'And you can keep your plasters and your bath, I don't want anything from you. In no way are you going to get me into your debt!'

'I'm afraid I'm going to insist,' he said, smiling grimly. 'But you needn't feel indebted. Let's say it's one of the perks of the job, free baths at the boss's house until your own facilities are complete.'

'For my father as well,' said Sherril tightly. In that way she would not feel he was favouring her.

'For Peter as well,' he agreed, surprisingly calmly, she thought. Perhaps he had realised that he was at fault for not ensuring their cottage was up to standard before they arrived.

Walking across to his house with him, Sherril felt selfconscious, aware that two of the stud hands were watching their progress with unconcealed interest.

In no time it would be all over the place that she had been into the boss's house. And it was not difficult to guess what interpretation they would put on it.

CHAPTER FOUR

THE inside of Nick Diamond's house was a revelation to Sherril. She had expected traditional grandeur, something Regency perhaps, with silver candelabra and striped satin curtains, formal dignified furniture.

Instead she was delighted by the welcoming warmth of the place. The main hall into which she stepped had a huge fireplace at each end, the stone floor was covered with occasional rugs in cheerful colours and a brass jardinière was filled with a charming disarray of honeysuckle and roses, spilling its perfume into the air. It was homely, and before she had gone any further she fell in love with the place.

'A bath first, I think,' said Nick, and led her up a wide staircase, that brought her out on to a square landing from which opened numerous doors. 'The one in the far corner's the bathroom,' he informed her. 'Take your time, pamper yourself.' The last two words were taunting and she flashed him a stony look before opening the door and shutting herself inside, sliding the bolt quickly, even though she had seen him making his way back downstairs.

The room looked as though it had originally been a bedroom. The walls and ceiling were beamed, finished with a rich medium brown varnish. The spaces between the beams were painted pink and the bathroom suite was beige. An immense mirror on one wall had a carved wooden frame, and the towel rail was of bamboo. A polished wooden cabinet housed Nick Diamond's toiletries, and there were a couple of old-fashioned water jugs and bowls on a marble-topped dresser on the other side of the room. In case the plumbing system failed, thought Sherril.

It was an unusual bathroom, a mixture of old and new, but an interesting one, and she realised with surprise that it suited Nick's personality. He was something of a mixture himself.

She turned on the taps, stripping off her clothes, dropping them into a heap in one corner. She was impatient for it to fill, anxious to rid herself of the clinging smell of horses.

Trying to recall the last time she had had a bath, the last time she had lain in warm scented water, revelling in the luxury of its silkiness against her skin, she discovered it seemed like an eternity. It had in fact been the day before they moved, a mere two weeks. She felt they had been here a lifetime.

Experimentally she tested the water with one toe and then slipped into its depths which smelled agreeably of the herbal bath salts she had discovered in his cabinet.

It seemed strange to her that she had never seen anyone else entering or leaving his house, yet obviously someone did his housework, and did it very well too. Perhaps he had a resident housekeeper. Perhaps, she smiled wryly, she too was a prisoner in this valley. Except that if it was a woman who had been born and bred in the Dales she would like it here, she would not complain as she, Sherril, did.

She lay for a long time, until the water cooled, until her thoughts became calm. Until she could forget that ravaging kiss that had moved her more than she cared to admit.

Before leaving the cottage Sherril had grabbed a dress and clean undies, and she put them on now, conscious that not only did she smell better, but she felt better. Her aches had melted away, only her hands were still tender, the plasters having released themselves not long after she climbed into the bath.

Down in the hall Nick Diamond awaited her. He looked her up and down, sniffed exaggeratedly, and said, 'That's better. How are your hands?' She held them out and he inspected them closely. 'They still need dressings, will do for a few days by the look of them. Come into the kitchen.'

Here again the emphasis was on natural materials. The floor once more was stone, work surfaces were quarry tiles and pine shelves housed an assortment of kitchen equipment. The only concessions to luxury were a washing machine and refrigerator.

Cooking was done apparently on a massive range set into an alcove at the far end. It was a big kitchen, as were all the rooms that she had so far seen, and Nick pushed her on to a bamboo and rattan chair while he reached into a huge medicine cabinet high on one of the walls.

Again, as he ministered to her needs Sherril felt an annoying quickening of her pulses, and held herself rigid. He had no right to affect her in this manner.

He frowned, but said nothing, moving away directly he had finished.

She looked at her hands ruefully, and as if following her line of thought Nick said, 'A convenient way of getting out of work tomorrow.'

She looked up at him indignantly. 'Are you insinuating that I did this deliberately?'

He shook his head. 'I don't think even you would be that stupid. I didn't realise what a soft young thing you are. I shall have to think of something else for you to do.'

'I thought I was supposed to be replacing Jim,' she said tightly.

'You were. I shall have to put one of the other men on it until your hands have healed. It's a nuisance, but I have no alternative.'

'You could do it yourself,' she dared.

'Or I could make you do it despite your blisters,' he cracked. 'Talk to me like that and I damn well will.'

His harsh tones angered her. 'That wouldn't surprise me—you'd probably make me do it on my knees if I'd hurt my feet.'

'I would,' he returned. 'I've no time for weaklings. You seem to forget that on the very day you arrived here you threw Women's Lib at me. What's happened? Are you a turncoat? No longer the liberated woman you professed to be?'

'I never said I wanted to work on your farm!'

'A lot of women do,' he said. 'I know plenty of women who can turn their hand to any job at the stables, who muck out as good as a man, better in fact.'

Sherril glared. 'I notice you don't employ any. If they're so good, why's that?'

He sighed impatiently, and raked his thick dark hair with his fingers. 'I happen to believe that men work much better without the distraction of female company.'

'Then why did you make me do it?' she flashed.

'I had no alternative. I was one man short.'

'But you're going to find someone else to do it now,' she said triumphantly.

'Am I?'

There was a light in his eyes that she did not like. Maybe she had gone too far. She knew he was quite capable of insisting that she do the loose-boxes again tomorrow, and she also knew that with her hands in this condition it would take even longer. Each movement with the fork would be painful, each time she lifted the barrow she would want to cry out.

'You said you would.' Her voice was less aggressive and she could tell by his face that he knew she was beginning to regret her outburst. It was enough to incense her again. 'But I'll do it, Mr Diamond. I should hate to give you the pleasure of seeing me give in.'

He looked surprised. 'Determination was not one of the characteristics I attributed you with. I like a woman with guts. Make sure you're there at seven-thirty sharp—oh, and try not to let it take you so long this time.'

Inwardly fuming, Sherril rose from her chair and crossed stiffly towards the door. 'Thank you for the plasters and the use of your bathroom. I can see myself out.'

It was not until she reached her own cottage that she realised she had left her dirty clothes behind.

She cursed silently, but was definitely not going back. He could keep them for all she cared.

He was impossible! How she was going to manage tomorrow she did not know, but some way she would do it, even if she rubbed every inch of skin from her hands in the process. No way would she let him gloat over her inadequacy.

Her father came in earlier than usual and Sherril was attempting to peel potatoes. She had pulled on a pair of rubber gloves, but it was awkward and she was not making a very good job of them.

'Here, let me do that,' said Peter Martin. 'Why didn't you wait?'

'You're not usually this early,' she said.

'But I knew the condition your hands were in,' he said. 'You know I wouldn't let you work while they're like that.'

'You ought to tell that to Nick Diamond,' she said crossly. 'There's no letting up so far as he's concerned. I'm to be there at seven-thirty sharp again tomorrow and no shirking.'

Peter looked disbelieving. 'He's seen your hands? Does he know what you've done to yourself?'

'Of course he knows,' snapped Sherril. 'He dressed them himself—oh, and before I forget, the builders are coming on Monday instead of next week, and Nick Diamond says we can use his bathroom until ours is ready.'

'It looks as though you've already taken him up on that offer,' he said, looking appraisingly at his daughter. 'But what's this about him making you muck out the stables tomorrow? I don't believe he could be so uncaring.'

'You don't believe anything about him.' Sherril placed the chip pan on the stove and reached a packet of frozen peas from the refrigerator.

'Because everything you tell me is totally alien to what I know him to be like. You rub him up the wrong way for some reason. I expect you've had words again, and in a fit of temper he told you you had to do it.'

'In a fit of temper *I* told him I would do it,' she cried, 'and being the gentleman he is of course he agreed.'

'He didn't mean it,' said Peter airily. 'I'll have a word with him later. I'm certainly going to take him up on his invitation to use his bath.'

'You'll do no such thing,' said Sherril hotly. 'He'll think I've been complaining. Promise me, Dad, promise me you won't mention it.'

He sighed and nodded resignedly. 'You know what you're playing at, but I'm blowed if I do. I think you're being silly. There's no need for this martyr act.'

There was a need, she thought, if only to keep her pride intact, but she could not expect her father to understand.

After their meal her father went over to Nick Diamond's house for the promised bath, and Sherril went to bed. She could not remember the last time she had gone so early, but with another hard day tomorrow she needed to build up her energy.

She woke some time later; it was dark, and she could hear her father talking downstairs. Frowning, she looked at the luminous figures of her alarm—it was just after midnight.

Wide awake now, she climbed out of bed, opened her door. The voices were much clearer, and it took but a few seconds to realise that the second man was Nick Diamond.

What was *he* doing here? If her father had said anything about her working tomorrow, after he had promised, she would murder him! For a few minutes longer she remained at the top of the stairs, but they were discussing Pasadena Lady, the mare who was due to foal, her father expressing concern over her condition.

She went back to bed, but did not fall asleep until she heard their visitor go and her father climb the stairs to his room. She was tempted to call out, ask why Nick had come, but decided to pretend she had not heard.

Her father woke her once again with a cup of tea, smiling broadly. 'No need to get up yet, love. Nick's changed his mind, he has something else for you to do.'

Sherril looked at her father with wide accusing eyes. 'You told him! And you promised. Why?'

'I said nothing,' he protested. 'Nick brought the subject up himself—said he had a job more suited to you.'

'What is it?' she asked suspiciously.

Peter Martin shrugged. 'He didn't say.'

'And who's going to muck out the stables?'

'We'll do it between us,' said her father off-handedly, 'that's what usually happens when someone's on holiday. If we all muck in,' he smiled at his unintended pun, 'it won't take long.'

'Not so long as it took me yesterday, I suppose you mean,' Sherril said bitterly, still not really believing that he had said nothing to his employer.

'You're not used to the work,' he said gently. 'None of us were quick to start with. I've had a lifetime mucking out, it won't be any hardship to me.'

'So long as you're not doing them all,' she said. 'I wouldn't be surprised if you hadn't suggested taking my place, only you're not telling because you know I'll be annoyed.'

He smiled. 'Drink your tea, love. I'll see you later.' At the door he turned. 'You're to go to Nick's house at nine, mind you don't go back to sleep.'

'Is that an order?' she asked, but he had already gone, and she was left wondering what Nick Diamond had planned for her.

Although it was not much after seven she got up and after washing and dressing ate a leisurely breakfast, listening to the radio. Afterwards she made their beds and cleaned away their breakfast things, then because there was still half an hour before she reported to Nick Diamond she limped across to Meg's, filling her in on all that had happened the previous day.

'I can't imagine what he has in mind,' she said, 'Something even worse than mucking out, I expect.'

Meg grinned sympathetically. 'Give the man the benefit of the doubt! It could be a cushy number, maybe he had a twinge of conscience.'

'That man's got no conscience.' Sherril glanced at her watch. 'I suppose I'd better go. Talk about bearding the lion in his den—now I know what it feels like.'

'You sound as though you're giving in,' said Meg. 'That's not like you.'

'Oh, I'm not, don't worry,' replied Sherril. 'It's just that I like to know what's in store.'

She rang the doorbell at nine precisely. Nick opened it at once, almost as though he had been waiting. 'Good morning, Sherril. I see you got your father's message.'

'What prompted you to have a change of heart?' she demanded abruptly. 'I hope my father didn't put in a plea on my behalf.'

'You complained to him, then?' Grey eyes gleamed derisively as he stepped back for her to enter.

'I told him the facts, I didn't object. I'm no coward, Mr Diamond.'

'So I'm beginning to realise, and since we're to work together why not call me Nick? Everyone else does.'

'Work *together*?' Sherril looked at him suspiciously. 'Just what is it that you've planned, Mr Diamond?'

He looked down at her hands. 'How are they this morning?'

'You've not answered my question,' she said tightly.

'I thought perhaps they would be able to hold a pen and maybe use a typewriter. Am I right?'

She nodded. It had never occurred to her that it might be anything like this. She was not so sure she wanted to work in such close proximity to this hateful man.

He wore grey slacks this morning, and shoes instead of the boots which were his normal uniform. His white short-sleeved shirt moulded itself to his muscular chest, revealing hard sinewy forearms.

'It's the day for my secretary,' he said, 'but he rang last night to say that he has 'flu, and is likely to be away for a couple of weeks.'

'*He?*' asked Sherril incredulously. 'And on a Sunday?'

Nick Diamond nodded. 'In case you hadn't heard, this is a totally male household. My housekeeper, whom you'll meet shortly, is as capable as any woman, and I also have a part-time male cook, who comes in when I'm entertaining, otherwise my housekeeper cooks.'

Sherril had seen enough of the house to know that he spoke the truth. The shine on the furniture was so deep you could see your face in it, there was not a hint of dust anywhere. The only giveaway factor, she realised now, was the flowers bunched into the jardinière. A woman would have arranged them more artistically.

'I see,' she said. 'You carry your maxim that no women shall be employed on the farm into your house as well. Is it yourself you're afraid will be disturbed by the female anatomy? Ought I to be on my guard or perhaps dress in more manly clothes?'

She had donned a pretty silk blouse this morning, in a heavenly shade of blue, and wore with it a white pleated skirt and white low-heeled sandals. She had known at the time of dressing, that it had been a ridiculous get-up, especially if he had some other manual work in mind, but she had been in a contrary frame of mind and now she was glad.

His eyes narrowed, and he looked at her insolently. 'No way will we get any work done if you insist on baiting me. I suggest we call a temporary truce to this private war you appear to be waging.'

'*I* seem to be waging?' Sherril was indignant. 'You're the one who started it. The day we met you bawled me out!'

'We won't go into that now,' he said tightly. 'Come, I'll show you where you're to work,' He led the way towards the wide staircase. Sherril began to follow and then checked herself when she saw where they were heading.

'My study is up there,' said Nick impatiently. 'I have no ulterior motives, if that's what's on your mind.'

Reluctantly she allowed him to precede her, not altogether sure that she trusted him. He opened the nearest door and she had her first glimpse of the room in which he did his work.

It was large, carpeted, cluttered, but comfortable. In front of the window was a huge oak desk, one wall was lined entirely with books, another housed a collection of paintings; that they were all of horses came as no surprise.

Once inside she saw that a photo-copier stood in one corner and several filing cabinets occupied another. There was a wooden-armed swivel chair before the desk and a deep chintz-covered armchair in the centre, next to an old table that groaned beneath the weight of innumerable books and magazines.

There was no sign of a typewriter or a spare desk. She wondered where she was supposed to work.

Nick handed her a notebook and pencil, indicated the armchair, and said, 'Are you ready?' When she remained standing, too surprised to obey, he continued impatiently, 'You can do shorthand?'

She pulled herself together. 'Of course, but I naturally thought you would first explain a little of what you want me to do.'

'You'll pick it up as you go along,' he said. 'For today I have a whole batch of letters that need urgent replies.' He picked up a sheet of paper from his desk. 'To Mr P. O'Connor, at the Limerick Stud in Ireland. Dear Mr O'Connor, I apologise for not replying to your letter earlier——' He looked crossly at Sherril. 'You've got that?'

Anxiously now she sat down, and soon her pencil was flying over the pages. He gave her no time to breathe, dictating at such a pace that it taxed her concentration to its fullest extent. She had not boasted when she said she was good, but this man worked like a Trojan, not letting up until he had replied to every letter in the pile.

She had not had time to look at her watch, and was surprised to find it almost one. Nearly four hours of sitting in one position had made her stiff and she stood with difficulty, flexing her limbs. 'I must get Daddy's lunch. I'll be back at two.'

He pushed himself up. 'You're having lunch here, I've already fixed it with your father. No sense in you running backwards and forwards every day.'

The housekeeper turned out to be a man in his late fifties, small but wiry with plenty of energy, and Nick introduced him as Blake. He had prepared them a cold chicken salad, followed by a slice of melt-in-the-mouth apple pie, which he assured Sherril, when she complimented him on it, was cooked by his own fair hands. He certainly was a treasure, there was no doubt about that.

Afterwards Nick showed her to a small room next to his study, in which there was a desk and typewriter and all the stationery she would need.

He left her then and a few minutes later she saw him reverse his white Range Rover out of the yard. She watched his progress along the ribbon of road that led out of the valley, until the vehicle was no more than a speck in the distance, eventually disappearing altogether

She could see now why he had chosen his study on this side of the house. He had a bird's eye view of all that was going on. At the moment the yard was empty, the stables having already been finished and every tell-tale wisp of straw swept away.

Nick Diamond was a stickler for cleanliness, that much was apparent. Sherril had never seen a place kept in such immaculate condition.

She let her eyes rove beyond the buildings, saw their cottage behind the trees and realised with a start that Nick could almost see right into it, making a mental note to remember to close her curtains before she started undressing at night.

Farther afield the green slopes of the valley were criss-crossed with the interminable drystone walls, disappearing over the horizon like columns of marching soldiers. There were occasional outcrops of bare limestone, deeply fissured by running water that glittered in the afternoon sun.

Some of the hands were repairing the fencing that surrounded the paddocks belonging to the Diamond stud. The mares were cropping contentedly at the grass, their foals running races with each other, but always returning to their mothers' sides, never wandering too far away, as if afraid they might disappear if they lost sight of them.

One of the mares was rolling on her back, her legs kicking towards the sun. Sherril remembered her father telling her that rolling to a horse is a way of grooming herself, to get rid of itches and sweat, and if she has been ridden, the smell of the person.

From this distance she was not afraid of them, in fact she quite enjoyed watching their antics. She wondered which of the mares was the progeny of Black Diamond and whether her foals would be surefire winners when they were eventually raced.

It was the first time she had taken any interest in horses, but some of the enthusiasm with which Nick had spoken had somehow transferred itself to her and it was all she could do to drag her mind back to what she was supposed to be doing.

Nick had said he wanted all the letters sent out that day, but as she got down to typing, pushing herself to the limit, she realised that the task he had set her was a sheer impossibility. No one but a superhuman being could type fast enough to finish that lot.

At six o'clock she decided to call it a day. The letters that she had completed she put in a neat pile on his desk, leaving her pad and the unanswered letters beside her typewriter ready for tomorrow.

Typing had exhausted her almost as much as mucking out the stables and she was glad to relax after she and her father had eaten their meal. 'I'm going across to Nick's house for a bath now,' he said. 'You just sit there, you look positively worn out.'

'I am,' said Sherril, and before long had fallen asleep in her chair. She woke suddenly, aware, before she even opened her eyes, that there was someone else in the room. Was it her father back already? Had she been asleep that long? Or was it someone else? A prickle down her spine, a sudden awareness, told her who it was.

She opened her eyes wide. 'What are you doing here?' she demanded querulously.

'More to the point, what are you?' His tone was harsh, angry, and she shot up.

'I happen to live here,' she said pointedly.

'I'm not referring to that. You haven't finished those letters. I distinctly told you I wanted them done today.'

'Are you trying to tell me that your secretary would have got them typed in one afternoon?'

'He would have stayed until they were finished, if I'd left instructions to that effect.'

Sherril tossed him a haughty glance. 'He sounds a marvel. But since it's Sunday, and there are no postal collections, I can't see what difference it will make if I finish them in the morning.'

'They can be on their way by then, if they're dropped into the postbox tonight,' he returned harshly. 'When I give orders, Miss Martin, I expect you to carry them out. You will be adequately compensated for the unsocial hours.'

'But not for the drag on my health,' she flung back. 'Typing is hard work, it uses as much energy as a man shovelling coal, in case you weren't aware of it.'

'I wouldn't dispute that,' he said smoothly, 'but you're accustomed to it, or so you assured me. If the job's too much you can always go back to mucking out.'

His insinuation made her say hotly, 'Of course it's not too much,' and his satisfied little smile told her that he had said that deliberately, and she reacted in exactly the way he had known she would.

'Then you'll have no objection to coming back with me now?'

She glared hotly, her green eyes flashing. 'I do object, I object most strongly, but I don't suppose I have much choice. You'll probably threaten me with my father losing his job again if I refuse.'

'I very well might,' he said.

'I somehow think it's an idle threat,' she returned strongly. 'I don't think you would go to that extreme, you're merely trying to frighten me.'

Thick brows rose. 'Try me, you'll soon find out.'

But she knew she couldn't, she daren't; her father's whole future was at stake and no way would she jeopardise that.

'Daddy's at your house now, isn't he?' she asked, 'having his bath?'

'If you're wondering whether you'll be adequately chaperoned, I don't think you need worry your pretty head about that. I have no designs on your virtue.'

'I'm glad to hear it,' she said tightly, and with a resigned sigh, 'Shall we go?' At least she had had the benefit of a few minutes' sleep, it had helped recoup her energy and she did not feel so tired as she had earlier.

At the top of the stairs they went their separate ways, Nick into his study and Sherril into the little office next door. She could hear her father splashing in the bathroom and it comforted her to know that he too was in the house.

Very soon she was completely immersed in her work and jumped when her father's voice sounded over her shoulder.

'I heard the typewriter,' he said. 'I thought you'd finished for today.'

'His Highness thought otherwise,' she said grimly. 'Another hour should do it and then I can come home, unless of course he decides to go on working through the night, I wouldn't put that past him.'

'Is that what you'd like?' Nick's face appeared in the doorway. He was quite clearly not pleased to hear himself being spoken about in that manner. His eyes were cold and distant, his mouth tense. 'It can easily be arranged.'

'It is not what I would like,' snapped Sherril, putting her hand to her aching neck and shoulders, 'but apparently I'm here to obey and if it's what you desire who am I to argue?'

'You're tired, love,' said her father, resting his hand on her head. 'Nick's teasing you, can't you see that?'

'Oh, no, I'm not, Peter,' returned the big man. 'Sherril deserves everything she gets from me. You've protected her for too long and now she's met someone who has no sympathy for her and she

doesn't like it. If you heard half the things she says
to me you'd want to crawl away in shame.'

'And if you heard what he says to me,' retorted
Sherril, not to be outdone, 'you'd soon realise he's
not quite the perfect gentleman you think!'

Peter Martin's lips tightened. 'You've said
enough, Sherril. Mr Diamond is my employer, in
case you'd forgotten, and as such deserves respect,
from you as well as me. I don't want to hear you
arguing again.'

Savagely she turned back to her typewriter. Nick
Diamond was always in the right to hear her father
speak. What was it going to take to make him realise
that his boss showed his daughter no respect, so why
should she look up to him?

She heard him ask Nick to take another look at
Pasadena Lady, who was still giving them cause for
concern, and then they disappeared.

Her peace of mind disturbed, Sherril found it
difficult to concentrate and letter after letter she tore
from her machine, screwing it into a tight ball and
slinging it into the waste bin.

She would have finished by ten had it not been
for their interruption, now it looked as though she
would be here until midnight.

She had just tossed her third attempt at a particularly tricky letter into the bin when the door
opened and Nick walked in. He looked over her
shoulder to see how she was doing, observed the half
full bin with narrowed eyes.

'How much longer are you going to take?'

'How the hell do I know?' demanded Sherril

crossly. 'It's your fault that it's taken this long. If you hadn't come in earlier I'd have had them done by now.'

'It upset you, did it, our little altercation?'

'Not upset,' she contradicted, 'I couldn't give a damn what you say, but it did disturb my concentration.'

'So I see. It looks as though you have half a box of headings in there. Do you realise how much it costs to have those things printed?'

'Are you suggesting that I pay for them?' Her voice was tight and it took all her self-control not to set about him. She would have taken great delight in slapping his face, shaking some of his self-control.

'No,' he said, 'not unless this sort of thing goes on and on. You assured me you were an excellent typist, a pity it takes so little to put you off your stroke.'

She glared. 'Doesn't your secretary ever make mistakes? Is he so perfect that he types each letter flawlessly the first time?'

'He's not bad,' admitted Nick. 'Of course, we don't have the flare-ups that you and I have, he has an even temperament, something desirable in a job like this, wouldn't you say? It's quite obvious to me that you can't cope when you're in a mood.'

If it wasn't for you I wouldn't be in one, she thought angrily, but she said, 'If you've quite finished, I'd like to get on. I have no desire to sit here until morning. Knowing you, you would probably insist that we begin tomorrow's work then, without letting me have a rest.'

'You're learning.' There was a mocking smile on

his face as he closed the door behind him.

For the next hour Sherril worked with determined concentration and eventually all the letters were finished. Nick's study was empty, so she put them on the desk, beside the others which he had already signed and put into their envelopes.

Somehow she couldn't see him taking them to the post office in Weirbrook tonight, even supposing he had the stamps. He had more than likely said that to force her into finishing them. He seemed to take a perverted delight in seeing her wear herself out.

She was about to let herself quietly out of the house when one of the doors in the hall opened. Light spilled on to the stone floor, accentuating its irregularities, and she looked across, startled.

Inside the room was her father, in the doorway stood Nick. 'I thought I heard someone. You've finished at last? Why were you creeping away, afraid I might burden you with more work?'

Her heated response died away when she saw her father's warning expression. 'I didn't want to disturb you,' she said lamely. 'I thought you might have gone to bed.'

'Without posting my letters? You should know me better than that, Sherril. As a matter of fact I wondered whether you'd like a ride into the village with me. You've been in the house all day, a little fresh air will help you sleep.'

She was so tired that she needed no help from any direction, and had her father not been there she would have told him so. But knowing that Peter would be upset if she bandied further words with h' boss, she shrugged. 'If you like.'

'Such enthusiasm,' Nick jeered, looking helplessly at her father.

Peter Martin smiled, unsure of himself, and stood up. 'I'll be going, then. I'll see you in the morning, Nick,' and to Sherril, 'Do you want me to wait up?'

'No need,' said Nick for her, 'I'll see her safely home. I'll go and sign those other letters.'

Left alone with her father, Sherril said, 'I shan't be long, Dad. I'm dead beat. If I had my way I wouldn't go with him, but——'

'But you're learning not to argue,' he finished. 'Good girl. I don't want to lose this job, it's the best one I've ever had. Nick's all right, if you know how to take him. You're too prickly, that's the trouble. He was right when he said I'd protected you too much, I can see that now. When you broke your leg I felt the blame lay with me for wanting to teach you to ride so early, and I suppose that ever since I've pampered you because of it.'

'It's because you love me, Dad,' smiled Sherril, 'and I love you, and no way am I going to lose you this job. I'll be nice to Nick Diamond if it kills me.'

The relief on his face was her reward, and he hugged her to him. 'That's my daughter! You're all I've got now, and I can't bear it when there's friction between us.'

'There'll be no more,' she vowed. 'I've made up my mind. Nick Diamond can ask what he likes, I won't complain.'

At that moment he returned, the pile of envelopes

fastened together with an elastic band. 'Ready Sherril?'

She kissed her father and followed Nick out to his Range Rover.

The powerful lights cut an arc into the night as they swung out of the yard and in a matter of minutes they were out of the valley and travelling along the main road towards Weirbrook.

The letters were on the seat between them and as Nick pulled up outside the little post office-cum-general store, Sherril jumped out and dropped them into the post box set into its wall.

Back in the vehicle she expected them to return home, and was surprised and a little apprehensive when he drove on through Weirbrook and along the road which she and her father had travelled the day they arrived.

'Where are we going?' she demanded breathlessly.

'To get the fresh air I promised you.' His head turned towards her and although it was dark she knew there was a taunting light in his eyes, that he expected her to complain.

Gritting her teeth, she sat very still, hands clenched tightly in her lap, her promise to her father uppermost in her mind.

For a few miles more he drove in silence, then pulled the vehicle off the road along a little used track. A hundred yards further he stopped.

They were high up. Sherril had not noticed that they had been gradually climbing, and all around them the land fell away. Above, the navy sky was filled with brilliant stars, and a pale moon hung suspended, as if watching over them, as if wondering what they were doing out here in this lonely place. Here and there the yellow lights of homesteads and farmhouses glittered, moonlight washed over the landscape. It was like looking down on earth from another world.

They climbed out of the vehicle and all that could be heard was the faint whisper of a delicate breeze brushing the grass at their feet. Sherril looked around her, entranced.

The breathless beauty of her surroundings heightened her emotions and she was intensely aware of the man at her side, wondering why he had brought her here. It was not long before she found out.

Almost imperceptibly his arm crept about her shoulders, holding her against him, so that she became aware of the vibrant beating of his heart. It echoed the urgent pulsing of her own, causing an upward surge of feelings so intense that they frightened her. Desperately she pulled away, but his other arm shot round and imprisoned her.

'I might have known you had some ulterior motive!' she snapped furiously. 'Let me go this instant, take me back to the cottage. I demand that you release me!'

He smiled and held her even tighter. 'Struggle all you like, my little wildcat. There's no one here to hear your cries.'

'You planned this,' she accused. 'Fresh air indeed! I could have had all I needed of that right outside your door.'

'Even an idiot would know that,' he agreed. 'So

when you willingly came I naturally assumed you were of the same mind. If your father hadn't stayed we needn't have made this little trek, we could have made love in the comfort of my home.'

'Made love!' Sherril's cry hung over the valley loud and clear, and frenziedly she renewed her attempt to escape, kicking and struggling, twisting her body. 'You've got a nerve, Nick Diamond!' she spat between one frantic move and another. 'I wouldn't let you make love to me if you were the last man on earth!'

His smile was clearly visible in the light from the moon. 'I shouldn't take a bet on that, if I were you.'

'I'd stake my life on it!' she yelled. 'I wouldn't allow any man who's treated me the way you have to lay one finger on me!'

He grinned insolently and lifted her chin with a firm finger. 'What am I doing now?'

She renewed her struggles. 'I've not much choice, but so far as anything else goes,' kicking his shin viciously, 'it's not on. I hate you, Nick Diamond, you know that, and——'

She got no further. Very effectively, clamping his mouth on hers, he shut her up, and no matter how she kicked or how desperately she strove to free herself, there was no way out.

His lips moved sensuously on hers, demanding, not letting up until she ceased fighting, not stopping even then, but less intense in their desire to draw a response, coaxing now and gentle.

When he felt her go limp his mouth moved from her mouth to trail a fiery course down the slim column of her throat, one hand cupping a breast, confident that she would resist no longer.

Desire flickered and flared, but fighting the instinct to respond, and taking advantage of his relaxed hold, Sherril wrenched herself free and ran away across the short, springy turf.

But she had not gone far when Nick did a flying rugby tackle from behind and brought her to the ground, his weight now imprisoning her so that it was absolutely impossible to move.

'You swine!' she cried. 'I don't have to take this from you!'

'If you ceased fighting there'd be no need.'

His breath was warm on her face and she felt a resurgence of a feeling which was now becoming familiar. She had to fight, *she had to*, otherwise she would give in, and where would it all end? What would happen between her and Nick? A cheap affair, a thrill on the side, for that was all it would be. There was no love lost between them, they had each made that perfectly clear.

In the end she did stop battling, not because she had given in, simply because she had used every ounce of strength. Nick was a powerful man, it would take an equal to fight him off, and no way was she any match for him.

Pressing home his advantage, Nick ravaged her mouth yet again, and as she lay there limply on the grass, Sherril's awareness of him grew and grew until in the end she found herself enjoying his kiss. It went very much against her better judgment to feel pleasure in anything this man did, but it was as though she no longer had any control over her feelings.

Expertly he parted her lips, exploring the soft moistness within, until she felt as though her whole body had turned to jelly and she was his to do with as he liked.

When her hands unconsciously crept behind his head, mingling in the wealth of dark springy waves, she felt him tense, then groan, then roll over so that they lay side by side. His hand slid inside her blouse, caressing, stimulating, until Sherril's breathing became ragged and she arched herself close. Pinnacles of desire she had never before experienced surged towards the surface and she desperately wanted him to make love to her.

No one had ever aroused her to such heights. She had had boy-friends in plenty, but their kisses could in no way compare with the expert touch of this man.

He was in complete charge of the situation, like he was everything else, she thought ironically, but strangely she did not seem to mind. It was as though she was floating on cloud nine, as though nothing else mattered, except that this man keep kissing her.

'Nick,' she heard herself say, and it was as if the voice did not belong to her, 'make love to me—please!'

CHAPTER FIVE

THE builders arrived early the next morning, and Sherril hurried from her bed when she heard the commotion beneath her window.

Her father had already started work, and she was alone in the cottage, enjoying an extra few minutes before she prepared herself for another day working for Nick Diamond.

When she heard his loud, authoritative voice combined with those of the workmen, she recalled vividly last night's scene, and went hot with embarrassment.

How could she? What must he have thought? The whole event flashed vividly before her mind's eye— herself begging Nick to make love to her, his own refusal. The humiliation.

And that dreadful drive home when he had not seemed in the least concerned, in fact she could not remember seeing him so relaxed and happy, and she had been on the edge of her seat with mortification.

Outside her cottage he had again pulled her into his arms, but this time she had refused to succumb to his persuasion, and dragged herself away with a smothered cry.

'Nine sharp in the morning,' had been his parting shot, as he put the Range Rover into gear and moved off into the yard.

Sherril stood a long time at her bedroom window, watching, wondering whether he too was looking towards the cottage. There was no way of knowing. No light shone out from the big house, and after a while she had crawled into bed.

Now she was afraid to face him again. Last night she had had the cover of darkness, in the clear light of day how could she look him in the eye without giving away her embarrassment?

Not that it made any difference. Whatever it was that had happened to her out there, it was still alive. She still desired him, craved the heady excitement of his body against hers.

Was it love? she asked herself. Had her hatred really been a disguise for these other feelings? Or was it pure physical attraction?

There was no doubt about it, he was a dangerously attractive male—when he set himself out to entertain, when he was not barbing her with insults.

Perhaps it would be better if they were still enemies, she thought to herself as she dressed, wishing she had had time to go down to the kitchen and wash thoroughly before the workmen arrived. At least then she had been able to keep him at a distance; now she did not want to fight, she wanted to be friends, hoped that one day Nick would make love to her.

In front of the builders he was distant and cool, but that was understandable; he would not want to let them see that there was any sort of relationship between himself and his stud groom's daughter.

It helped Sherril, too, to overcome her humiliation

and by the time she went over to his house she felt fully able to face him without revealing her feelings.

She had anticipated that he would be as warm and friendly towards her as he had been last night, was disturbed to discover that he was still coldly withdrawn.

Her assumption that his attitude had been solely for the benefit of the builders had been wrong. Somehow, since parting last night he had had a change of heart.

Perhaps it had something to do with her begging him to love her. The more she thought about it the more convinced she became that this was the case, and the deeper grew her shame.

Nick had a pile of filing ready for her and several documents to be copied, which meant that she had to work in his study. Nick himself sat at his desk.

'I shall be out this afternoon,' he said suddenly. 'There's a horse I want to watch race. If she's as good as I think she is I intend putting in an offer.'

'Haven't you enough mares?' asked Sherril.

He looked surprised. 'I'm always on the look out for new bloodstock. Besides, I don't intend to breed from Dark Velvet again. She's twenty-one and has dropped a foal regularly each year since she was five. I think she deserves a rest.'

Sherril recalled her father telling her that the secret of good horses was pedigree, and she knew that Nick Diamond only bought the best. She surprised herself by realising that she would have loved to go to the races with him, see this horse that he was so interested in.

But in his present mood she knew there was no way that she could ask, and he would certainly not invite her.

'There's a stallion standing at the Limerick Stud,' he continued. 'If I buy this mare I intend sending her for covering next year. Between them they should produce a winner. They both have excellent pedigrees.'

'Covering?' asked Sherril. She had heard her father use the expression but had never been sufficiently interested to ask what it meant.

He quirked a brow. 'Mating, Sherril,' and he watched her face closely, not missing her heightened colour, enjoying her embarrassment.

'I see,' she said quietly, and turned back to her filing.

She knew that he too was remembering her plea last night, and she wished she knew why he had denied her. He had been as passionately involved as she herself and it must have taken every ounce of his willpower to push her away. It could be, she supposed, that his conscience had bothered him, that he had not wanted to involve her in an idle affair. Or perhaps knowing that he could have her had been sufficient. Maybe that was what he had set out to do in the first place?

The notion made her go cold and she glared at her employer's back. If that had been the case he must be laughing up his sleeve right now. He had well and truly made a fool of the girl who professed to hate him.

Suddenly she could not stand being in the same

room with him. Ramming the rest of the filing back into its basket, she opened the door.

Nick called to her as she was about to close it again. 'Where are you going?'

'To the bathroom,' she invented quickly, 'if you've no objection?'

He ignored her sarcasm, merely nodding. 'Don't be long. I want that filing done before I leave.'

'I'm sure it's not that important,' she said heatedly. 'I can finish it this afternoon.'

'I have other work for you then,' he rapped. 'If you thought that because I shall be out you can take things easy you're mistaken.'

She slammed the door, feeling a rekindling of her hatred, and a certain conviction that whatever her feelings for him had been they were certainly not love.

She paid a quick visit to the bathroom and then went downstairs to the kitchen. 'Oh, Blake,' she said, glad that the housekeeper was there, 'have you any aspirin? I have a violent headache.' And she was not lying. It had been slowly developing all morning and Nick's few harsh words had turned it into a raging pain.

Blake looked at her sympathetically. 'You look pale. Sit down a moment. Would you like some hot milk?'

She nodded, glad of a few minutes' reprieve away from that hateful man. But she had been there for no more than a few seconds before Nick came charging in. 'What are you doing here?' he demanded.

'The young lady has a headache,' explained Blake. 'I'm making her a drink. It looks as though she could do with some fresh air.'

Don't mention fresh air to me, thought Sherril grimly. I had enough of that last night!

Nick looked sceptical. 'Are you sure it's not an excuse to get out of a boring job? I know no one likes filing, least of all myself, but it's a necessary evil.'

'Of which I'm fully aware,' she snapped, 'and yes, I do have a headache, and as soon as I've had my tablets and a drink I shall be back. I'm no slacker, Mr Diamond, I don't think you can accuse me of that.'

Their eyes met and locked in silent battle and Sherril was glad she was angry, because otherwise she knew what those smouldering eyes would have done to her.

Even so she was the first to look away, accepting gratefully the mug of warm milk and swallowing the aspirin Blake silently handed to her.

'I'll have some coffee while I'm here,' said Nick, 'and I'd like lunch early today, I'm going to Pontefract.'

Blake nodded. He was a man of few words, thought Sherril, in Nick Diamond's presence anyway. No doubt he was someone else who valued his job and knew better than to bandy words with his employer.

She was relieved Nick did not follow her back to his study, and she had finished both the filing and duplicating when he eventually returned.

He handed her a pile of papers. 'I want you to take the relevant data from these and enter them on to the cards in that cabinet,' he said. 'You'll find them perfectly self-explanatory. It's a new system I've started for checking pedigrees, but unfortunately it's fallen rather far behind.'

After lunch he disappeared, but not before he had made sure that Sherril had returned upstairs and begun work. She resented his attitude, his fear that if he did not stand over her she would shirk her duty, and before he went she said crossly, 'Are you going to phone later on to make sure I'm still at it, or do you trust me sufficiently to know that I shan't stop until I have finished?'

'If you do,' he said, 'I shall fetch you back, it's as simple as that. But perhaps I ought to warn you, in case you do feel like slipping away early, I shall be back between four and five. Make sure you're here.'

'And if I finish before then?'

He looked doubtfully at the sheaf of papers. 'I doubt it. I very much doubt it.'

Sherril did too. There looked enough work to keep her going for the rest of the week, and as the after-noon progressed she became more and more bored. The work was tedious, needing all her concentration to extract the vital pieces of information and fill them in in the appropriate places on the cards.

After an hour or so she stopped for a rest and was surprised to notice that the sky had clouded over. Since coming here she had seen nothing but blue skies, now it looked as though rain was imminent.

Her first thoughts were that it would stop work on the new bathroom, her second how it would affect the racing at Pontefract. Would the horse in which Nick was interested race to the best of her ability, or would he be disappointed and change his mind about buying?

Even as she watched it began to rain, big heavy spots which covered the ground in no time, streaming down the window so that her vision became blurred.

From the stables came a whinny of fear, and Sherril was puzzled. The horses were usually in the paddocks at this time of day, but even if one had been left behind for some reason there was no need for her to be frightened of the rain.

Then she recalled her father's concern over Pasadena Lady and wondered if the mare was in trouble. She had no idea where any of the men were. From her vantage point she should have been able to see them, but the paddocks and yard were empty, apart from the horses standing in clusters, unworried by the torrential rain.

Again the mare called out and Sherril decided that she had better go in search of her father. But although she checked all the outbuildings she could find neither him nor any of the men.

It was strange, there was usually someone about. Had they all decided to play hookey because Nick Diamond was away?

Cautiously now she approached the looseboxes, tracked down the one in which Pasadena Lady was nervously pawing the straw. Her eyes were anxious and she was sweating profusely.

It was the bay, the one who had been in her stable the day they arrived, and compassion filled Sherril that she should be alone at a time like this.

Although her knowledge of horses was negligible she knew enough to realise that the mare was in labour. She should be in the foaling block and someone with her.

She began talking softly, offering words of encouragement, her own fear forgotten for the moment. Frequently she glanced over her shoulder. If only someone would come!

The bay, as if recognising that Sherril was doing her best, moved forward and hung her head over the door, nuzzling Sherril, almost as if she was asking for help, asking why she was suffering.

'I'm going to move you into the foaling block before it's too late,' said Sherril softly. She was no longer scared of the horse. This was someone who needed her, who was more frightened herself and asked only for relief from the pain that was troubling her.

Opening the stable door, she grabbed a handful of the horse's mane and led her slowly out. It crossed her mind that Pasadena Lady, being driven crazy by this thing inside her, might decide to bolt, and could lose her foal as a result.

But it was too late to worry about that now. Luckily the mare walked docilely at her side and soon they were entering the foaling block which was ready for the event.

Once inside the bay's legs crumpled beneath her and she lay on the thick bed of straw, her head moving uneasily, her eyes glassy with pain.

Sherril knelt beside her, talking, stroking her neck, very much aware of the movements inside the horse, of the foal striving to escape, and Pasadena Lady's muscles working hard to expel it.

She tried not to think what would happen if the foal was born while she was here alone, she had no idea what she must do.

Suddenly there was a commotion outside and Nick strode in, followed closely by her father. When he saw Sherril curled up in the straw with the horse he was for a moment taken aback, but the next second he was beside her, his hands expertly feeling the horse's body.

He was infinitely gentle and he spoke softly to Pasadena Lady who, recognising him, became still for a minute, looking trustingly at the big man, her eyes begging him to make the pain better.

Pushing herself to her feet, Sherril stood back, watching, admiring Nick's technique, seeing how much more easy the horse had become in his presence.

'Where were you?' she asked her father quietly. 'I searched everywhere.'

'I went with Nick,' he said. 'We never expected her to start today.'

'And the others? I couldn't find anyone.'

'I know Jack wanted to fetch his mower, whether they went with him, I don't know. We've just been told that there's been an accident this side of Weirbrook, a lorry jackknifed and it's blocking the road. If they're the other side of that it might be hours before they get back. Nick's not pleased, I can tell you.'

Sherril could understand it. Each of his mares was worth thousands of pounds. If anything had happened to any of them, Pasadena Lady in particular, he would have been livid. Even now, she would not like to be in their shoes when they got back.

Nick was wiping the sweat from Pasadena Lady's skin with a towel, murmuring words of comfort, re-

gardless of the fact that he wore a good suit and a
pair of highly polished leather shoes.

'Did you bring her in here?' asked Peter Martin,
as he and Sherril stood watching, feeling helpless,
but knowing there was nothing they could do.

She nodded. 'I knew she'd be more comfortable,
and there's every facility. I forgot I was frightened,
she came like a lamb.'

He placed his arm about her shoulders. 'I'm proud
of you, love. You did very well.'

'It had to be done,' she said. 'I didn't think twice
about it.'

Nick stood up and took off his coat, rolling up his
shirt sleeves. 'It'll be a few hours yet, but I'm going
to stay with her.'

'Shall I send for the vet?' asked Peter.

'I don't think so.' Nick studied the horse, who
had struggled to her feet and was tossing her head,
pawing constantly, trying to get rid of the violent
disturbance inside her. 'Not unless there are complications. It's the first time she's foaled, she doesn't
understand what's happening. If only we could tell
her it will be all right soon!'

Outside the rain still sheeted down, falling on the
roof of the building like thunder. 'Can I make you a
drink?' asked Sherril, 'and perhaps a sandwich if
you're going to stay.'

He looked at her as though he had forgotten she
was there. 'Thanks, Sherril, I'd appreciate that. Put
my coat on or you'll get soaked going across the yard.'

She picked it up and slung it over her head and
shoulders before scurrying back to the house. Blake was

nowhere about, she guessed he had gone for the day.

While waiting for the kettle she buttered bread and cut thick slices from a freshly cooked ham which she found in the refrigerator.

She was almost afraid to take her time, not that there was anything she could do to help Nick, but she wanted to be there for the birth. She felt involved now, as though she could take a little bit of the credit, and her old fear of horses seemed to be very much a thing of the past.

Had it not been raining she would have taken their tea over on a tray, as it was she filled a flask and wrapped the sandwiches in foil, packing them into a basket that she found in the pantry.

Nick had resumed his position at the horse's side. He looked as distressed as Pasadena Lady and Sherril knew he did not like seeing her in pain. But there was nothing he could do.

Thoroughbred horses were sensitive, she had heard her father say many times, and poor Lady was no exception. But all they could do was wait, try to calm her, try to reassure her that soon all would be well and she would have her own foal by her side.

The men ate their sandwiches gratefully, and drank their tea. Sherril, despite the fact that she was hungry, merely nibbled at one. There was too much happening for her to eat. Afterwards, she promised herself, when the foal was born, when Lady was rid of pain.

She wondered whether women went through as much as this horse seemed to be doing, then recalled her mother saying that no matter how bad the pain it was immediately forgotten, and rejoicing in a newly born child was adequate compensation for any distress.

It would be the same with Pasadena Lady. How she wished she could communicate with her! She was so intent on watching the horse that she had not realised Nick was speaking to her.

'Come here,' he said, 'and listen carefully. Tell me what you hear.'

She knelt near him, her ear attuned to the horse's side. A look of wonder spread over her face. 'The foal's heartbeat,' she said breathlessly.

'And he's raring to be free. I've seen more foals born than I can remember, but I never fail to find it very moving. If it's a girl I shall name her Sherril, after you, because you've been very brave. It must have taken a great deal of courage to bring her in here.'

Nick's praise made her grow warm. 'I forgot I was frightened,' she said huskily, 'and now I don't think I am any more.'

He smiled and drew her to him, holding her for a few moments, but then the horse moved convulsively, violently, and all his attention was turned to the poor, pain-racked animal.

Her father helped him mop up the sweat and she wished there was something she could do. She felt so helpless.

There was a noise in the yard and Peter went out. Sherril heard his voice raised angrily, guessed that the rest of the hands had returned. But what her father was saying would be a mere taste of the wrath they would get from their boss. If one of them had

gone and got delayed it would not have mattered
but for them all to leave together was the worst thing
they could have done.

Time went slowly as her father and Nick took it
in turns to comfort the tormented beast. She half
expected them to tell her to go, was ready with her
plea that she be allowed to watch this wonderful
moment.

Jack and Sam popped their heads round the door
but withdrew quickly when Nick threw them a mur-
derous look.

Sherril poured more tea which they drank eagerly
before resuming their vigil at the animal's side. She
sat down in one corner, well away from the men, but
where she could see everything that was going on.

Gradually the rain ceased and through the high
window streamed the first watery rays of the sun.
Looking outside a short time later Sherril saw steam
rising from the yard as it quickly dried. Everywhere
smelled fresh and sweet and she inhaled ap-
preciatively before turning back into the tension-
filled room.

Pasadena Lady suddenly struggled to her feet
racked by a violent convulsion. Nick was unable to
do anything for her now. He nodded to Peter. The
time had come.

Sherril watched in agonised silence, feeling for the
horse, wondering why they had to go through all
this, afraid that she might injure herself because she
was straining so strongly.

When her tail lifted and the foal appeared Sherril
clapped her hands to her mouth and stopped

breathing. Please, God, let it be all right.

Nick immediately went to its aid, guiding the foal gently down on to the straw as Pasadena Lady's muscles worked furiously, freeing its protective membrane so that the head was clear, cleaning out its mouth and nostrils.

Her father filled a bucket with warm water and sponged down Pasadena Lady, who was looking at the foal curiously, as if to say, 'Where did that come from?'

Once the foal was clean and dry she struggled to stand, but had worked so hard to come into the world that she had no energy, and subsided weakly back on to the straw.

Spellbound by it all, Sherril could do nothing but stand and stare. The little animal was absolutely fascinating—perfect in every feature, an exact replica of its mother.

The foal made several more attempts before finally managing to stand and for the first time she saw her mother, staring at her as curiously as Lady had stared at her offspring.

They drew together and the mare licked the top of the tiny animal's head, knowing instinctively that it was her own, that she belonged to her and this was what all the pain had been about.

The foal nuzzled for something to drink and before long was sucking hungrily, and the three of them stood back and watched.

Nick grinned. 'Sherril, meet Sherril.'

'The two most beautiful women in the world,' said her father.

'The others can finish in here now.' Nick turned, satisfied that all was well. 'We'll go to the house and clean up.' His shirt was sweaty and bloodstained, and there were streaks across his brow where he had continually drawn the back of his hand. Straw clung in his hair and on the rough material of his trousers.

Sherril had never seen him look so weary, but he was happy. There had been none of the complications that her father had feared. Mother and daughter were doing well.

Before finally leaving the block, Sherril hugged the tiny foal, who had exhausted herself and was now back down on the straw. 'You're a little beauty,' she said. 'I wish you were mine.'

'I'll make a deal with you,' said Nick, who had overheard. 'You learn to ride and she's yours.'

Still on her knees, Sherril looked up at him, her eyes wide and troubled. 'You can't do that, she's worth far too much. If I had the money I'd buy her, but you can't give her away.'

'I mean it,' said Nick. 'You learn to ride and I'll be happy to let you have her. You've conquered one fear, now the only obstacle is getting on to horseback again. I want to see you do it, Sherril.'

'So much that you'd forfeit Pasadena Lady's foal?' She looked at her father, silently asking why he thought this man was making such a ridiculous offer.

Peter shrugged. 'You'll never get another chance like this, Sherry love. Take him up on it. I would if I were you.'

'I wouldn't ask you,' grinned Nick. 'Sherril's far

prettier. Come on, let's get washed and changed. You can give me your answer later.'

But Sherril was unsure of herself. It had been easy to look after Pasadena Lady, she had needed her, but to actually ride, that was another thing, and when her father and Nick came back downstairs she was still tossing the problem about in her mind.

To her amazement Nick wore jodhpurs. 'There's no time like the present,' he said smoothly. 'Run along and get yourself into a pair of jeans. I'll saddle the horses while I'm waiting.'

'I'm not sure that I want to,' she said. 'Can't we wait? I don't want to do too much in one day.'

He began to look cross. 'No, we can't wait, and your father agrees. Just think about the new foal. All horses were like that once, try and see them in that light and you need never feel afraid.'

'Easier said than done,' she replied mutinously.

'If you don't go and get ready I shall drag you there and change you myself!' Nick's eyes were glinting silver. 'So far as I can see it's a case of now or never.'

'I'd rather it be never,' she said defiantly.

'Right.' Nick grimly took hold of her arm and marched her out of the house, his grip not slackening until they reached her cottage. He let her go then. 'Do I have to come upstairs as well, or have you decided it's not worth fighting? I'm going to win, you can rest assured, so if I were you I'd take the easiest way out—and get changed—*now*.'

The worst part about it was that she knew Nick was right. Today was the best time, while she was

still feeling quite mellow about horses, before she ha
time to rebuild her old fears.

She changed quickly, but her hands were trem
bling and inside she felt all worked up. Nick ha
gone to saddle the horses and she walked hesitantl
back towards the farm.

When she saw him he was sitting astride a mag
nificent hunter. She hesitated, but then saw th
smaller Dales pony standing quietly beside him an
did not feel quite so nervous.

He dismounted and came towards her, and with
out giving her time to think put his hands on he
waist and swung her up into the saddle as thoug
she were no heavier than a child.

Her feet found the stirrups and he adjusted then
also pulling in the girth which had become slac
'Ben has a habit of blowing himself up when he
saddled,' he explained. 'Remember that when you'r
riding him alone, always check his girth after he
walked a few steps, otherwise you'll find yourse
hanging under his stomach.'

When she was riding him alone!

There was not much chance of that. She was onl
riding now because Nick had given her no choic
but her heart was beating painfully and her palm
were moist.

Nick remounted his own horse. 'Ben's an obedier
pony,' he said. 'He'll not throw you, so you nee
have no fears. We're going to take it steady this fir
time out, just a quiet walk, that's all. Ben will follo
when I move, he used to belong to a riding schoo
so it's instinctive. Just sit tight and let him plod alon

t his own pace. Okay?'

Sherril nodded. Her mouth was dry and the blood ounded in her head and the ground looked an wfully long way down.

When they began to move an unreasonable fear)se in her throat and she felt close to panic, but)on she became used to Ben's steady gait and when 1e realised he was not going to throw her she began) enjoy the feel of the horse beneath her.

The world was viewed from a different angle, and)on her grip on the reins relaxed and she began to)ok around. The rain had revitalised the tired-look- 1g grass and everything looked fresh and bright, lmost as though it was spring.

Nick turned off the road and they made their way cross the fields, Ben warm and comfortable. They avelled like this for about three quarters of a mile, ick frequently looking over his shoulder, enquiring hether she was all right.

When he reined in his mount Ben obediently opped, standing quite still, neither dropping his ead to crop the grass or moving away as Sherril ared he might. She patted his neck. If she had een given a pony such as this to learn on instead of 1e spirited horse who had objected to her sitting n his back, she might have been an accomplished orsewoman by now.

'Had enough?' Nick smiled warmly, encourag- 1gly, and her heart flipped. He had forgotten his l-humour of this morning and become once again 1e man she had begged to make love to her.

The two horses rubbed noses, the big chestnut and

her smaller dark brown one. They at least had n
inhibitions. She wished she could as easily lift he
head for Nick's kiss.

'I'm enjoying it,' she said. 'Ben's sweet. I've neve
known a horse with such a kind temperament.'

'You haven't given yourself a chance.'

'I suppose not.'

'We'll go back now, though. No sense in overdoin
it your first time out.'

'Do we have to?' She looked disappointed.

He grinned. 'I think so. But we'll trot, if you like
Ben's got a lovely smooth action. Remember to rid
up and down with him and you won't go wrong
He laughed when he saw her face. 'It's not difficul
and you won't have to tell Ben what to do, he'
follow me. That's why I put you on him. He's a
ideal pony to learn on.'

Leaning towards her, he curved a hand round th
back of her neck, pulling her forward and kissin
her firmly.

A chorus of angels sang in Sherril's head and i
that moment she knew that whatever Nick told he
to do she would oblige without question.

'Perhaps that will help,' he said.

She nodded, not realising the blissful expressio
that had appeared on her face.

He smiled complacently and urged his horse for
ward.

CHAPTER SIX

NICK regularly took Sherril riding after that, but each day, before she did anything else, before breakfast even, she insisted on paying the new foal a visit.

She had more than a normal interest in the animal, feeling she had contributed in some small way to her coming into the world, and as the baby horse gradually got to know her, trotting up as soon as she approached, nuzzling her hand for the inevitable titbit, Sherril became more and more attached, and very soon began to wonder why she had thought all horses vicious brutes.

Ben was a darling, and Lady Sherril, as she had eventually been named, was the loveliest foal in the whole world. Sherril sat for hours in the loosebox with the foal's head on her lap, whispering all sorts of nonsense, intended for her ears alone.

Sometimes she declared her growing feelings for Nick. 'You're very lucky to have an owner like him,' she told the foal. 'You could have someone who's not half so kind or thoughtful or loving.'

'Do you really mean that?' Nick's voice came over the stable door.

She looked up, startled. 'You shouldn't have been listening!' she said indignantly.

He pushed open the door and came inside. From

her position on the floor he looked taller and broader than ever. He was not handsome in the true sense of the word, but there was a virile ruggedness about him that she was finding more and more difficult to resist.

'But since I did hear,' he insisted, 'I want to know whether you were sincere.'

She smiled impishly. 'Of course I was. You treat your horses with the utmost kindness.'

'That wasn't what I meant.' His voice had deepened and he joined her on the straw, not for one moment taking his eyes from her face. 'Do *you* find me kind and thoughtful and—er—loving?'

She did. *She did.* But how could she tell him, and why was he asking? Admittedly he had been much nicer of late, taking great pains to help her overcome her fear of horses.

But whether he felt anything more than a genuine desire to help, she did not know. He had not kissed her again, though there had been times when he looked as if he would like to, almost visibly restraining himself.

She had wanted him to kiss her, had longed for his embrace with a desperation that shocked her. But only Lady Sherril had been told the true state of her feelings.

'I think I love him,' she had whispered one day and the foal had looked at her with her big brown eyes and Sherril had been quite sure she understood.

'Or,' Nick continued, when her answer was not immediately forthcoming, 'do you still consider me a bigheaded, arrogant swine—the original male chauvinist? Those were the words, I believe?'

Had she really called him that? Swift, humiliating colour flooded her cheeks. 'You must have thought me awfully rude.'

'I thought you more than that,' he said, 'but I won't embarrass you with it.'

'And have you changed your opinion of me now?' she enquired coquettishly.

He smiled. 'Let's say you're the one who's changing. I've noticed you feel less sorry for yourself these days.'

'That's because I have something to occupy my time.'

'You could have worked from the beginning, but you were so dead set against me I thought it best not to force the issue.'

Sherril's eyes widened. 'I don't believe that. You made me muck out those stables.'

His smile was rueful and he picked up her hands, studying them closely. 'If I'd known what it was going to do to you, I wouldn't have insisted.'

The blisters were healed now, all that was left were the fading marks. She watched, fascinated, as he gently pressed a kiss into each palm.

He had said that she was changing, but it was nothing compared with the difference in him. He had been as hard as nails to start with, yet now he treated her as though she was someone special, as though she meant something to him!

Their eyes met and they stared at each other for a long time, until at last with a groan Nick gathered her into his arms. The foal was forgotten as she returned his kisses.

They lay back in the straw, hungry for each other, kissing with a desperate kind of savagery, as though this was the last chance they might get of expressing their feelings for one another.

He lay half across her, imprisoning her. Not that she wanted to escape. She loved him, and wanted him, and when he lifted his head, stroking back the hair from her face with infinite tenderness, she linked her hands round his neck and pulled him down again, her lips meeting his eagerly.

Her heart beat an ecstatic tattoo within her breast, her body arched convulsively and she strained herself against him, needing him desperately, never having felt this way about any other man.

It was difficult to remember that she had once hated him, once sworn she would never love him, not in a thousand years. Now she knew it would break her heart if he was playing about with her, if he did not return her love.

When at length he pushed her from him she tried feverishly to cling, but quite firmly he released her fingers. 'Much more of this,' he said, 'and I won't be responsible for what happens.'

'I don't care,' she cried, but inside she knew that she did, and because Nick was behaving like a gentleman she loved him all the more. Had he let their lovemaking reach its inevitable conclusion she knew that later she would have been filled with remorse, felt ashamed, most probably have hated him and laid the blame on his shoulders.

He pulled her to her feet and she stood there while

he plucked the straw from her clothes, her eyes not once leaving his face. She loved every line on it, every tiny wrinkle, and she reached out and touched him, her love welling up in her throat, threatening to choke her.

'Sherril!' The word came hoarsely.

She licked dry lips. 'Yes, Nick?'

'Let's get the hell out of here.'

It was not what she had expected, but she followed him blindly.

'Go and have your breakfast,' he said, 'and I don't think you'd better come up to the house today.'

Disappointment crushed her. 'Why?' Was he already regretting what had happened? Was she mistaken, did he not feel the same way? Had he merely kissed her because he thought it was what she expected?

'I don't feel in the mood for working,' he said bluntly, 'and I don't think you're in any fit state either.' With that he left her, striding quickly towards his house, leaving her to limp slowly back to the cottage.

It was empty, her father having already begun work. Sherril sat down and began to cry, then scolded herself for being an idiot. It was quite plain that Nick did not return her feelings. He desired her physically, but that was all, and she should be thankful that he had not taken advantage.

Their bathroom was finished, and she went up now, half filling the bath with water. It was a plain white suite, nothing like the luxury of Nick's bathroom, and the walls were tiled in sunshine yellow.

She intended buying orange curtains when she eventually managed to get someone to take her on a shopping expedition, but for the moment the frosted windows were bare.

Nevertheless, it was a boon to have their own bathroom, she had been surprised how quickly the workmen had completed it, and she sat in the water, soaping herself thoroughly, trying to wash away the erotic feelings aroused by Nick Diamond.

She did not know which was the worst, unrequited love, or sworn enemies. They both had their drawbacks, but at least life was easier when they were friends. She would simply have to learn to hide her feelings.

But Sherril felt no better when she was washed and dressed, and unable to face the thought of food she went again to Lady Sherril's stable. The foal was greedily sucking her mother's milk.

'You don't know how lucky you are,' said Sherril. 'Life's so simple for you. Be thankful you're not a human with all the trials and heartache that go with it.'

The young horse finished drinking and came across to Sherril, nosing her affectionately while Pasadena Lady watched every movement. She wrapped her arms round the foal's neck. 'You're so beautiful,' she said. 'I love you almost as much as I love Nick.' Then she looked over her shoulder anxiously, scared in case he had once again crept up on her.

Nick had made no further mention of presenting her with the foal, but since she had learned to ride she supposed that theoretically she was hers, and if Nick could not accept the love she held for him, then she would bestow it on this tiny animal. The foal at least appreciated the interest shown in her.

The morning passed slowly. Sherril wanted to go up to the house but was reluctant to defy Nick's orders. He had wanted to make love to her, she knew that, and admired his self-control, fully aware that this was the reason he had banned her from his house today.

She wondered what would happen if she went. Whether he would be angry and throw her out, or whether his sexual desires would get the better of him and they would end up in bed.

But she did not want it like that. She did not want a cheap affair. She wanted Nick to love her as she loved him.

Standing by her bedroom window, she looked across, knowing exactly which room was his study. When she saw a movement inside she knew that he too had been watching the cottage.

On an impulse she decided to take Ben out. She needed to get away from Nick, away from the temptation of going up to the house and opening her heart.

Fetching his saddle and bridle from the tack room, she went round to the stable where he was normally kept. She had forgotten that he would be out in the paddock and for a moment felt foiled when she saw the empty loosebox.

But determined now to carry out her plan, she trekked down to the field, hanging the saddle on the

fence while she went to fetch Ben. She surprised herself by venturing into the paddock which housed not
only the placid Dales pony, but several other mares
and fillies as well.

Her steps were hesitant at first, but gradually, as
she realised that none of them would harm her, that
in fact they were more afraid of her than she was of
them, she walked confidently to the far corner where
dark brown Ben was cropping contentedly.

She had thought to pop a carrot into her pocket
and held it out now in the palm of her hand. He
came happily enough, allowing her to slip on his
head collar and lead him from the field.

She tacked him up and climbed on to his back,
her heart beating a little quicker than normal when
she urged him forward. This time he had not Nick's
big chestnut hunter to follow and she wondered
whether he would obey her commands, or whether
he would suddenly develop a mind of his own.

But all was well and they trotted confidently along
the narrow road. After a while Sherril forgot her
fears and began to enjoy the ride. Ben obeyed her
slightest touch.

They crossed the stream in the valley bottom, the
pony stepping delicately through the shallow, quick-
running water; they climbed the hill on the far side,
pausing to look back at the Diamound stud, then
cresting the brow dropped down again through
sparsely wooded banks and ramparts of rock.

Sherril had been this way with Nick and Ben
needed no telling, following the route faithfully,
pausing when he thought his rider wanted to admire

he view, walking slowly over the rougher areas, rotting gaily when the going was even.

At one time Sherril urged him into a canter, exhilarating in the feel of the wind rushing through her hair, laughing aloud with sheer enjoyment. They were travelling unexplored ground now and she pressed him even harder. But her laughter changed into a loud shriek as Ben came to an abrupt halt and she went sailing over his head.

The ground rushed up to meet her, memories of that other terrifying time flashed vividly before her mind's eye, and then all went black as the breath was crushed from her body.

When Sherril came to she was cradled in Nick's arms. 'Darling Sherril, wake up,' she heard him say. 'Oh, my love, please speak to me. I'll never forgive myself if anything happens to you!'

For a few seconds she lay there, fully conscious now, but purposely keeping her eyes closed, wanting to hear what else Nick had to say.

'Sherril, I love you. Oh, God, it's all my fault! I should never have urged you to ride again. Sherril, please say something, *please*!'

Nick loved her!

It was what she had wanted to hear above all. If it had taken a fall to make him say it then it was worth the pain that was filling her head right now.

Very slowly she allowed her eyes to flicker open, closing them again quickly as the brilliant sunlight hurt. But Nick had seen and he bent his head, kissing her brow lightly. 'Sherril, can you hear me?'

She nodded, but the pain increased, and she

winced and lay limp in his arms.

He groaned and muttered an oath. 'It's my fault! How could I have been such a fool to let you ride alone! How much are you hurt, Sherril? Can you move?'

Her green eyes were filled with pain as she looked at him. She lifted her hand. 'It's my head,' she whispered, touching it gingerly.

Carefully he examined the spot she had indicated, cursing anew as blood stained his fingertips. 'You've got a deep cut. You must have hit your head on a boulder. I pray to God you've done no serious damage.'

Her vision became blurred as he gently lifted her and she felt herself passing out again.

The next time Sherril opened her eyes she was in bed. Nick sat on a chair at her side, her hand in his, an anxious expression on his whitened face.

'How are you feeling?'

'I have a headache,' she said. It hurt even to look at him, each movement of her eyes making her aware of the pain, and she closed them again quickly.

She had been dreaming, she had dreamt that Nick said he loved her. It was a wonderful dream, the culmination of all her hopes. Again she glanced at him and what she saw in his eyes told her that it had been no figment of her imagination.

'Darling Sherril,' he said softly, his voice full of suppressed anguish.

In that first brief second she had seen the love shining from his eyes. They were veiled now, compassion only filling them, but it had been enough for her to know the depth of his feelings.

Lifting his hand to her mouth, she pressed her lips against it. 'I love you too, Nick.'

He looked as though he could scarcely believe it. 'You don't know what you're saying. It's that knock on your head.'

'I do know.' Her voice became stronger. 'And I do love you. Hold me tight, Nick, tell me again that you love me.'

He complied readily, taking care not to jolt her as he lifted her into his arms. 'Dearest Sherril, I love you so much, I thought I'd die when I saw you fall off Ben.'

'You saw me?'

'I followed,' he admitted, 'at a discreet distance. I was proud of you, do you know that? So proud. At last, I thought, she's conquered all her fears.'

'What made Ben stop?' she ventured.

'I should have known when I saw you heading in that direction. I ought to have warned you.' He was angry with himself. 'Some picnickers left a white plastic bag of rubbish there once and it flapped in the breeze, startling Ben. He bolted, and ever since has been nervous of this spot.'

'Poor Ben,' said Sherril.

'Poor you!' exclaimed Nick. 'You could have been killed!'

'But I'm not.' She managed a weak smile. 'All I have is a lump on my head and a splitting headache. I'll be as right as rain in a day or two.'

'The doctor's calling,' Nick said. 'He might want you in hospital. Bangs on the head are funny things.

You don't know what other damage it might have
done.'

'I won't go,' declared Sherril, clinging tightly to
Nick.

'I don't want you to, my love. I never want to let
you out of my sight. But we must do what the doctor
says.'

With that she had to be content. 'Kiss me, Nick,'
she begged, when he lowered her back again to the
pillows.

'Are you up to it?' A tiny frown creased his brow,
his grey eyes were all concern.

She touched his lips with her fingers, following
their strong lines, her eyes devouring him. With
every passing second she felt stronger.

With a groan he lowered his head, kissing her
carefully, afraid in case he hurt. But Sherril wanted
more. She linked her hands behind his head and dis-
missing the pain which surged with ever-increasing
intensity, quite unashamedly clung to him, her lips
parted invitingly, and Nick was a lost man.

Neither of them heard the door open and Sherril
looked across selfconsciously when a voice said,
'Well, my patient doesn't look as though she's suffering too badly!'

Nick, not in the least perturbed to have been
caught kissing Sherril, said smoothly, 'Dr Raistrick,
glad you got here so quickly.'

'And this is the young lady who got thrown?' The
balding doctor smiled broadly. 'I'm not so sure that
Mr Diamond's cure isn't better than mine.'

She blushed and glanced across at Nick, who was

also grinning. 'She's hurt her head,' he said. 'Quite a nasty cut.'

The doctor examined the wound thoroughly, asked Sherril several searching questions while he carried out various tests. Then he said, 'I don't think it's anything to worry about. Keep the wound clean and I'll give you some tablets for the pain. They might make you a bit sleepy, but that's all to the good. Keep a close eye on her, Nick, over the next few days. Give me a ring if there's any setback, no matter how slight, but I don't anticipate any problem. Give her a week and she'll be up and about and on horseback again.'

Sherril met Nick's eyes, knew exactly what was going through his mind. But this time she was determined not to be put off by a fall. Her father had told her often enough in the past that you had to fall off twenty-four times before you could ride.

'Before then I hope, doctor,' she said pertly, feeling a surge of warmth at the pride and pleasure on Nick's face.

As the doctor left her father came in. 'Sherril love, how are you, what have you been doing?'

'I'm fine, Daddy, just fine,' and she grinned like a Cheshire cat.

'You certainly look better than I imagined,' he said. 'When I got the message that you'd fallen from your horse and hurt your head, I died a thousand deaths. If anything should happen to you, my precious, I don't know what I'd do.'

'I'll look after her, Peter,' said Nick, 'never fear. She'll come to no harm.'

Sherril's father looked questioningly from his employer to his daughter, sensing a change in their relationship. 'Is there something I should know?'

Nick glanced at Sherril, for once in his life seeming a trifle unsure of himself. He then turned back to her father. 'Peter,' he said, 'I'd like to marry your daughter.'

This was quite obviously the last thing Peter Martin had expected. His brows shot up and his mouth fell open. He glanced at Sherril and back again to Nick. 'Have you two been holding out on me?'

Sherril was as surprised as her father, but overcame it more quickly. 'We—we've only just discovered that we love each other.' She glanced up at Nick and beckoned him to her. 'As a matter of fact he's not even asked me if I'll marry him!'

'Then perhaps you'd better give him your answer first.'

Sherril's heart beat a tattoo within her breast. She found it difficult to believe that she had heard Nick correctly. It was all happening so speedily. It was like a fairytale, like a dream come true.

Nick sat on the edge of the bed and took her face between his hands, tenderly kissing her eyes, the tip of her nose, and finally her mouth.

She gazed at him adoringly and knew that she had no need for words. Nick knew as surely as she did that she would marry him tomorrow if it were possible.

'I do want to marry him, Daddy,' she said.

'Then you both have my blessing.' Peter looked

close to tears. 'I know it's a corny saying, but it's true all the same. I shan't be losing a daughter but gaining the son I've always wanted.' He held out his hand to Nick. 'Congratulations, you're a very lucky man.'

'I know,' admitted Nick. 'You sang her praises to me so often before we met that I feel I've known her for years. If it's all right with you, Peter, I'd like the wedding to be soon. I can see no sense in waiting.'

'If it's agreeable to the bride,' smiled her father.

Sherril closed her eyes. It was all becoming too much for her. She was not sure whether she was awake or dreaming.

'We'll discuss it later,' said Nick quietly. 'Poor Sherril's tired out. I think we're both forgetting that she's ill. I'll keep her here, Peter, if you don't mind. You can move in too, there's plenty of room.'

Their voices faded and Sherril slept and when she woke it was dark. A lamp on her bedside table filled the room with shadows. She had at first thought she might be in Nick's bedroom, but now realised it must be one of the guest rooms.

It was too pretty to belong to Nick. The dark beamed ceiling was counteracted by light flowery chintzes covering the bed and hanging at the open window.

A light breeze chased its way inside, caressing her face, disturbing a vase of flowers, bringing with it the smell of horses and roses and that indefinable something that was the Dales.

With surprise she realised that she had come to love the Yorkshire **Dales,** almost as much as she did

Nick himself. She could now contemplate her future here with no qualms at all. So long as Nick was at her side she felt she could remain in this valley for the rest of her life, without once fretting for the sort of existence that she had once lived.

The door opened and Nick came in. 'At last!' he said. 'I was getting quite worried. You've slept for hours and hours.'

'I had a dream,' she smiled. 'I dreamt you wanted to marry me.'

He returned her smile, gently touching her face. 'And what was your reaction?'

'I was given no choice.' Her eyes were tender, challenging, and as she had known he would do he bent down and kissed her soundly.

'Very proper,' he said with mock severity. 'Women were put on this earth to do man's bidding.'

Sherril's eyes flashed. 'Nick Diamond, I may not be in complete control of my faculties, but I do remember that I hate male chauvinists, and if you continue——'

She got no further. His mouth closed on hers yet again, possessively, passionately, demanding and getting complete response. 'There's no backing out now, Sherril my girl. You take me for better or worse.'

'Until death us do part,' she completed, with a silly smile on her face. 'Oh, Nick, I do love you, and I'm glad I fell, otherwise I'd never have known that you love me.'

'Don't you believe it,' he said. 'We'd have got

round to it one day. It was on the cards. It was all a matter of which route we took, a short direct one, or a long stormy one.'

'But you despised me so much in the beginning. When did you decide that you loved me?'

'I never hated you.' His voice was sincere. 'I thought you were thoroughly spoilt and I wanted to take you down a peg or two, right up until that time you mucked out the stables, keeping at it even though your hands were sore and bleeding. Then I knew you had courage, that you weren't the ruined little darling I'd imagined.'

'And that's why you asked me to do some secretarial work, not because my father had said anything?'

He nodded and kissed her again. 'I was so angry with myself when I saw your hands. You have no idea. I wanted to take you into my arms there and then and confess my love.'

'What stopped you?'

'Because you weren't ready to accept it. You were still fighting me. You hated my guts. Have you forgotten already?'

Sherril smiled ruefully. 'I did hate you, Nick. I thought you were the most loathsome man who walked this earth.'

'You didn't want to come here and you took it out on me.'

She nodded. 'I'm sorry.'

'So you should be. It will take an awful lot of loving to make up for all the pain you've caused. And talking of pain, how's your head, my darling?

You're making me forget you're not well.'

She had forgotten herself. 'It's much easier,' she said. 'Those tablets are good. I have a slight headache, but nothing like the one I had earlier.'

'Are you hungry? Blake's prepared you a light meal, he'll be most hurt if you don't do it justice.'

'I'm starving,' declared Sherril in surprise.

Nick disappeared, returning almost immediately with a tray containing an appetising assortment of fresh fruit and salad and cold roast chicken, and a glass of yellowish-looking mixture. She looked at it askance.

'Egg whisked in milk,' he said. 'Blake assured me that if you ate nothing else that alone would do you a power of good.'

'Where's Daddy?' she asked between mouthfuls. 'I heard you telling him he could stay.'

'He prefers the cottage,' said Nick. 'But he'll be in shortly. He's popped in and out so frequently today I fear he must be neglecting his work.'

'But you don't mind because it's me,' she said confidently, smiling across the tray and marvelling that this gorgeous hunk of manhood could have fallen in love with her.

'Look at me like that,' he husked, 'and I'll be in bed with you whether you're ill or not.'

It felt good to be loved, and she finished her meal happily, drinking down the egg and milk, which tasted far nicer than she expected.

'There's one thing I must apologise for,' said Nick when she had finished, 'and that's the state of the cottage when you moved in. I really had no idea

Bert had let it go, and if you hadn't been so aggressive I'd have asked Blake to clean it.'

'But you thought it would do me good,' she nodded, not quite able to hide a smile. It didn't matter any longer, nothing mattered, except that she was safe and happy in her new-found love.

The pain in her head was returning and Nick, attuned to her every mood, gave her another tablet, then turned out the lamp and left.

In no time at all she was asleep again.

The next two days passed in a hazy round of sleep and pain and happiness. Nick or her father were always there when she needed them, and if ever she had been spoilt in her life it was now.

On the third day she woke feeling more like her normal self. Apart from a tenderness at the back of her head and a little niggling headache she felt as though she had never been ill.

Her days in bed had taken their toll, though, and when she got out her legs buckled beneath her. She was like Lady Sherril, she thought, recalling the moments when the foal had been born.

She was still smiling at the comparison when Nick came in. 'You're looking very pleased with yourself,' he said. 'I take it you're feeling much better?'

'I feel fine,' she nodded, 'but my legs won't obey me. I was thinking that I'm like Lady Sherril the first time she tried to stand.'

'I can carry you,' he said, swinging her into his arms before she had time to realise what he was doing. 'Where do you want to go?'

'I need a bath,' she said, 'and then I'll get dressed and come downstairs.'

'A bath it is,' he grinned, and proceeded to carry her into the bathroom. Gently he put her down, then turned on the taps, lavishly tipping in scented salts.

She expected him to go when the water was ready, and was surprised when he turned and said, 'Shall I help you with your nightdress?'

'No, thanks, I can manage,' she said stiffly.

But still he did not leave. Instead he leaned back against the wall, his thumbs hooked into his belt.

'You can go now,' she said evenly. 'I shan't need any help.'

'I'd prefer to stay,' he replied. 'You're still not fully recovered. I should hate you to pass out in the bath. Besides, if it's your modesty you're concerned about, remember that I'm your future husband and as such we should have no secrets.'

'We're not married yet,' snapped Sherril. 'You have no rights at all.'

Nick pulled a face. 'I thought your enforced rest might have improved your temper. I see I was wrong.' But he was not annoyed, instead he pulled her into his arms, kissing her tenderly, a kiss which told her that he loved her, which was full of suppressed desires.

'I've wanted to do that for days,' he said, 'but I've been afraid almost to touch you, you looked so frail. I'm glad you're better, Sherril.'

'Me too,' she murmured, her mouth against his, her heart racing. She felt lightheaded and knew that this time it was not entirely attributed to her accident.

His hands caressed her, intimately possessing, and r the moment everything was forgotten. It never eased to amaze her that he had asked her to marry im and she felt proud that he had chosen her. urely a man such as him could have his pick of any girls.

Not that she had ever seen him date anyone else, r even mention one. He led an almost monastic life ere at the stud, and suddenly she wondered why. Without thinking she said, 'Nick, have you ever had ny other girl-friends?'

It was a stupid question, she realised that the moment she had spoken. Of course he had had girls, is sexual expertise told her that.

'Jealous?' he grinned, and then, 'I've had my hare. Any particular reason why you ask?'

She shrugged. 'Not really.'

'Feminine curiosity, I suppose, but since we're to e married perhaps I should confess.' He still held her, ut his hands had stilled and there was a haunted ook on his face that she had not seen before.

She recalled her father once saying that there had een a woman in his life who had let him down adly. 'You don't have to tell me,' she said quickly. t was an idle question, I'm not desperately con-erned.'

'Then you should be,' he said, half laughing, half erious. 'I know all about you.'

'From my father, I suppose?' She was glad she ad no guilty secrets.

'I tell you what,' he said. 'You climb into your ath and I'll fill you in on my sordid past while you cleanse your beautiful body. I shall enjoy that.' And before she could object he had slid her nightdress from her shoulders so that it fell on the floor at her feet.

Automatically she crossed her arms in front of her, glaring crossly. 'You had no right doing that!'

'I have every right,' he said softly, deliberately moving her arms and allowing his eyes to slide over her rounded breasts, her slim hips and flat stomach.

'You're even more beautiful than I expected,' he said in a hushed kind of voice. 'I'm a very lucky man.'

He made no attempt to touch her again and some of her shyness subsided, to be replaced by an ache, a longing to be possessed. Her breathing deepened and became ragged and Nick said thickly, 'Get into the bath before—before it gets cold.'

Sherril knew that that was not what he had intended saying, and her love overflowed until she was filled with a wanton desire that shocked her.

'There was a girl once,' he said, his back to her now as she climbed into the water. 'I was very much in love with her, we planned to marry.'

He stopped and was so deep in thought that Sherril thought he had forgotten he was speaking to her. 'What happened?' she probed softly.

'Vanessa was an only child, and spoilt, a little like you—or like I thought you were—but I could put up with that. It was her greed for personal possessions that put me off. It took me a long time to realise that she was only after my money. I showered er with gifts, a horse of her own, a new sports car, wellery, furs, everything she asked for she had.

'It wasn't until she demanded I buy a house in ondon that I realised she would never settle here, hat she had pretended to like it, but that all the me she had had her sights set on moving me away.

'She couldn't stand the country, I discovered that hen we had our last final row. She told me in no ncertain terms what she thought of my stud farm.

dead-and-alive hole, she called it. Am I glad I idn't marry her! It would have been the biggest iistake of my life.'

Sherril had listened sadly and now she said, 'How o you know you won't be making a mistake marry-ig me? I too am from London. I loved the life here.'

He smiled confidently. 'Past tense. You love it here ow. I've watched it growing on you. Oh, you fought at first, you rebelled like any true townie, but I've ot noticed it bothering you of late.'

'That's because I love you,' she said simply. 'I ant to be where you are. I don't care whether you o to the ends of the earth, I'll follow.'

'I expect sometimes you'll want to get away,' he aid, 'and I shall willingly take you. You'd become cabbage shut up here month in and month out. I lso intend teaching you to drive, and you shall have our own car, then you can come and go as you lease.'

'You're good to me, Nick,' she said humbly. 'I on't deserve it.'

'You deserve the best of everything,' he returned.

'I love you, Sherril, and don't you ever forget that
It was the best day's work I ever did when I per
suaded your father to come and work here. He'd
shown me photographs of you, do you know that? I
think I fell in love with you before I met you.'

'But you hadn't realised what a terror I was?'

'A divine terror,' he smiled. 'A spunky little thing
who wasn't afraid to stick up for herself. I admired
you from the beginning. All I hoped was that your
hate campaign wouldn't last too long, I don't think
I could have waited much longer.'

'If I hadn't returned your love, what would you
have done?' she asked mischievously.

'Gone slowly mad,' he replied. 'But you're not
counting on my devious charm. I could get any
woman to fall for me if I set my mind on it.'

'You certainly didn't go out of your way to get
me to fall for you!'

'Because I didn't want a repetition of the Vanessa
affair. You were too much like her for me to take
any risks.'

'And do you think you're taking a risk now?' she
enquired, her eyes dancing with impish humour.

Nick looked at her threateningly. 'You're taking a
risk, talking to me like that. You're in a very pre-
carious position, young woman, and if I were you
I'd behave.'

She picked up the sponge and flung it at him and
he retreated. 'I can see you'll need a very firm hand,'
he said, as he closed the door.

Sherril smiled and sank low into the water. Oh,
she was happy, so very, very happy.

CHAPTER SEVEN

DURING the days that followed Sherril could never remember feeling so contented. Nick insisted she remain at the house, even though she assured him that she was completely recovered, and he pampered her ridiculously.

He was totally alien to the man who had greeted them on their first day at the stud, and she marvelled at the difference.

Her father too was happy. He clearly approved of her marrying Nick, and there were times when she wondered whether he hadn't had this in mind all along.

Nick wanted him to live with them at the house, but Peter's independent streak made him refuse. He preferred the cottage, he said. He had his meals at the house, but that was all.

While Sherril was ill Blake had gone across and done her father's cleaning, but now she was better he insisted on doing it herself.

'I don't know why you won't let me go back and live there,' she said to Nick one day. 'I feel guilty leaving Daddy on his own.'

'Peter doesn't mind,' he said confidently, 'and I want you where I can keep an eye on you. I've had enough of your hare-brained schemes. They always end in disaster. Besides, he might as well get used to the idea of you living here.'

And Sherril did not argue, she was quite happy about the whole thing.

She began to do Nick's secretarial work once again, but he worked her not nearly so hard, insisting she take plenty of rest, and after a while he encouraged her to ride Ben again.

At first she felt apprehensive, but gradually her fears evaporated and after a couple of times out her confidence returned and Nick took her on longer rides. Often they galloped, letting the horses have their head, and Sherril found it a most exhilarating experience.

Nick congratulated her on her progress, never pushing her too far, always watchful, always ready to stop if he thought she had had enough.

One evening, Nick and her father and herself were having dinner, when Nick said, 'I think it's about time we discussed the wedding.'

She had wondered when that would come up, had been afraid, for some reason she could not put her finger on, to broach the subject herself. She smiled at him lovingly. 'I seem to remember you saying there was no point in waiting, or did I dream that?'

Had she dreamt the whole thing? Although Nick treated her with every tenderness he had not brought up the subject since the first day she had got out of bed. She glanced down at her bare hand. Wouldn't he have given her an engagement ring if he had been serious?

There was no disputing the fact that he loved her

ough, and he caught her glance. 'Does it mean
at much to you? If you're so bothered we'll go into
ork tomorrow and buy the biggest and best ring
e can find.'

She shook her head, her worries dispersing. 'So
ong as I have you I don't care about a ring.'

'That's what I thought.' His warm smile en-
eloped her and she found his hand across the table.

'I do love you, Nick,' she said.

'If you'd like me to go,' laughed Peter.

'Dearest Daddy, don't you dare!' Sherril turned
er affections to her father, getting up from the table
nd throwing her arms round his neck. 'I'm the
appiest girl in the whole world, and I don't care
who sees it.'

His smile was contented and proud and he said, 'I
eckon the sooner you fix that date the better. I don't
vant to interfere, but if neither of you have any
bjections I'd like it to be on September the first.'

'Your anniversary!' Sherril suddenly remembered.
That would be nice, we'd like that, wouldn't we,
Nick?'

He nodded. 'We certainly would, Peter. I can't
hink of anything nicer. How long does that give us,
hree weeks? Think you can get your trousseau ready
n time, Sherril?'

'If someone will drive me somewhere *civilised* I can
et it ready in a day.'

She dodged Nick's playful slap. 'How long would
ou have been married, Daddy?'

He looked sad. 'Twenty-five years. We'd planned
. party.'

Sherril bit her lip, for a brief second her old hatred of horses flashing back. If it hadn't been for one of them her mother would be alive now, and they would be celebrating, and—she wouldn't have met Nick! They say that some good always comes out of disaster, and she consoled herself with this thought now.

She tried to smile cheerfully. 'Never mind, Daddy, you can celebrate our wedding instead.'

'A pity your mother won't be here to see you. I know you'll make a beautiful bride. She'd have been so proud.' With an effort he forced himself to be cheerful again. 'But I mustn't be morbid. You're happy, and that's all that matters to me now. At least you won't be moving away. That was something I was dreading, being left on my own.'

Nick said, 'Your home is with us, Peter, for the rest of your life.'

Two days later Nick drove Sherril into York. She was fascinated by the city, by the narrow streets, the medieval and Jacobean architecture, the walls that girded the old city, but above all by the Minster that dominated it.

Nick told her that it was the largest Gothic church in England and dated from the thirteenth century. 'But,' he continued, 'its origins go back to a tiny church which was built here when St Augustine came to convert England to Christianity in the year 597.'

Sherril was not particularly interested in history but could not help being awe-inspired by it all. They took a brief look round the cathedral, Nick saying that she could not visit York without seeing inside its famous Minster.

The medieval stained glass windows exploded with a riot of colour and light, and she learned that they were classed among the art treasures of the world. They were certainly beautiful; she had never seen anything quite like them, and was completely taken up with the large east window which, she was told, was reputed to be the largest area of stained glass in the world, depicting scenes from the Old Testament and the Book of Revelations.

Her visit left her feeling tranquil and very humble and she was silent as they made their way back through the streets.

Nick smiled and held her hand, completely attuned to her emotions, but when he took her into a jewellers she soon forgot her peaceful mood, exclaiming aloud as tray after tray of rings were brought for her examination.

'They're all so beautiful,' she said. 'You pick for me, Nick, I can't make up my mind.'

He slid on a ring with a central diamond surrounded by emeralds. 'To match your eyes,' he teased. 'It was accompanied by a wedding ring that matched the bark effect of the gold. 'A perfect pair,' he said, 'like you and me.'

Sherril forgot the assistant and gazed lovingly into his eyes, letting him kiss her with tender passion. In a dream she was led from the shop, and decided it was a good thing she had done the rest of her shopping beforehand.

The wedding dress she had chosen, insisting that

Nick remain outside while she selected, was in a Victorian style of heavy Nottingham lace, which made her feel demure and innocent, in complete variance with the wanton feelings he managed to arouse in her.

She had also purchased lots of frivolous undies and nighties and a silk jersey two-piece for wearing after the wedding. Nick had not mentioned a honeymoon, she was not sure he could spare the time, but just in case she added a few dresses and sandals and a couple of swimsuits.

It was a once-in-a-lifetime occasion, she assured herself, when she thought of her depleting bank balance, and as Nick had said that everything else would be paid for by him she had no regrets, her biggest desire to make him proud of her.

Back at the house she could not wait to show Meg her wedding dress. The other woman had been overjoyed to hear of their engagement, and Jack had admonished a cautious, 'I told you so.'

Sherril had pulled a face at him but hadn't cared that he had been right all along. She was far too much in love to care what anyone said.

The nearer the the time came for their wedding the more apprehensive Sherril felt. She was ecstatically happy, so happy that she was afraid it would not last. It was too good to be true, and she found it difficult to concentrate on the work Nick gave her.

Her normally perfect typing became full of errors and in the end Nick said, 'Sherril, my sweet, I know you love me, and I know your mind's full of the wedding, but work has to go on. Do you think you could try to type my letters correctly?'

She bobbed out her tongue impudently, but said, 'Perhaps you ought to get back your secretary. I'm sorry, Nick, you have this effect on me—I can't help it.'

He pulled her into his arms. 'And so it should be. I want you to tremble at my touch, I want you to beg me to make love to you, I want——' He groaned and crushed her against him. 'I want you in my bed, dearest Sherril. How much longer do I have to wait? I'm a tortured man, don't you know that?'

Their lips met and wave after wave of vibrant passion washed over Sherril. Had he carried her to his room there and then she knew she would not, could not, refuse.

It was almost violently that he pushed her from him. 'I must be patient,' he said, and it was as though he was talking to himself. 'Leave those letters, I have something else I want you to do.'

She followed him into his study and he fetched from his drawer a huge catalogue of horses. Every horse that he had ever bred was there, with a photograph and full details, to whom it had been sold, what had happened to it since, everything.

'I want this bringing up to date,' he said, fishing out a pile of photographs which were waiting to be mounted. 'You'll find the name of the horse on the back and the details have already been entered. It's a simple job, it won't tax your mind, you won't have to concentrate so much as you did on the typing.'

He grinned and she lunged at him. He caught her wrist and kissed her again. But this time it was a brief, hard, kiss and within seconds he had gone.

For a few moments Sherril did nothing but stare into space. She had never known that falling in love could be like this. It had completely taken her over, she did not feel like her own boss any longer, she belonged to Nick, utterly and completely, and when he was not here she felt bereft.

From the window she watched him cross the yard, tall and proud, his dark hair gleaming, his booted legs powerful. He stopped to say something to Sam, they laughed, and then he carried on until he was out of sight behind the stables.

Sherril bent her head to the work he had given her, sorting through the photographs, smiling at a particularly appealing young foal, realising that he had only given her this task now because she had got over her dislike of horses.

To have asked her to do this job in the beginning would have been torture. In fact she would have refused, more than likely ripping up the photographs. Now she looked at them with genuine pleasure, sticking each one into its appropriate place until at length she had finished.

There were some very famous horses indeed here, she realised, as she flicked back through the pages, all bred by Nick, though she had not been aware of it before.

She knew he took his work seriously, made a big thing out of studying lineage and only bought the best bloodstock, having his mares covered by notable stallions so that the resulting foals were on to a winning thing from the word go.

Suddenly her eyes became glued to the page in front of her, she felt herself grow cold, prickles ran down her spine and her heart beats accelerated. Fury built up inside her.

She closed the catalogue, then opened it again, her breathing ragged and fast, her breasts heaving as she struggled with her emotions.

Nick had bred the horse!

The horse. The horse that had killed her mother.

Her fists clenched on the desk in front of her. Why hadn't he said? He must have known. Had he kept it to himself because he'd known she'd be furious?

The longer she stared at the page, at the distinctive white markings on the black horse, the angrier she became.

It was almost as though Nick himself had killed her mother. She was beyond rational thought, all her old hates and fears returning.

He had calmly told her he loved her, calmly planned to marry her, all the time knowing that it was his fault her mother had been killed.

No wonder he knew so much about the accident. He had bred the horse, knew exactly how she would react under the circumstances—*and yet still he had not told her*.

Did her father know? Had he too hidden this terrible secret, or had Nick kept him in the dark as well?

Her palms were clammy, her mouth dry, and her breath rasped in her throat. She slammed the book, unable to stare at its tell-tale pages any longer.

Wrenching off her ring, she threw it on the desk and

with sobs tearing at her breast she fled the room.

It was all over. No way could she marry Nick after this. She raced across the yard and along the lane to the cottage, rushing up to her old room and flinging herself down on the bed.

How long she lay there she did not know. She wished she could cry, but no tears came, only great racking sobs that hurt her chest, and she wished she had never heard of Nick Diamond.

It would have been better had she not known. It wouldn't have helped the fact that her mother had died unnecessarily, but it would have saved her the torture of having loved a man who was the indirect cause of the accident. Who had kept a dark, guilty secret from her, had even agreed to their marrying on her parents' anniversary without so much as a twinge of conscience.

It was late when she heard the door of the cottage open and she tensed herself, up there in her bedroom. She had become calmer, her anger had slowly dissipated, to be replaced by an ice-cold hatred a hundred times worse than anything she had felt before.

She tensed herself, waiting, knowing that it was Nick come to find her. He called from downstairs. 'Sherril, are you up there? Sherril! *Sherril!*'

Knowing that sooner or later she would have to face him, she slowly dragged herself from the bed. 'I'm here, Nick,' and her voice sounded unlike her own.

He took the stairs two at a time, entering her room like a tornado. His brow was dark, his grey eyes furious. In his palm he held her ring. 'What's the meaning of this?'

She stiffened and backed until her legs touched the bed. 'I've changed my mind.' How could she sound so calm when inside she was filled with loathing, a desire to lash out at him, to beat him from the room?

'You've changed your mind?' A pulse jerked in his jaw, his face was paler than normal. 'And I have to accept that without explanation?'

'Yes.' She strove to face him, but there was hurt as well as anger on his face and she was afraid, and looked away. Deep down inside she still had some feeling for him, but knew that it must be stamped out, no way must it surface and sway her judgment.

'I'm damned if I will!' In two strides he was across the room and she was in his arms, his mouth on hers.

A betraying weakness rose in her and she struggled desperately to escape. She had to be strong, this thing was too terrible for her to even contemplate giving in to the desires Nick was still capable of evoking.

With a superhuman effort she wrenched free and ran to the door. She swung it wide. 'Keep your hands off me, Mr Diamond! Get out, get out now!'

She thought he was going, but it was only to take the door from her nerveless fingers and close it again. He leaned back against it, arms folded across his broad chest. 'Suppose you tell me exactly what's going through that tiny mind?'

'I don't have to tell *you* anything,' she snapped. 'I

have my reasons, that's all that matters.'

'Not to me it doesn't. One minute you're incapable of resisting me, I could have taken you to bed this afternoon, now you're staring at me as though I'm someone completely abhorrent. I want to know, Sherril, and I want to know now.'

It would not help matters if she told him, so what was the point? She shrugged. 'You'll wait a long time.'

'You mean you refuse to tell me what's brought about this change of heart?'

She nodded.

Nick swore violently and the next second left the room. She heard his feet thundering down the stairs and the door close with a bang which shook the cottage.

Crossing to the window, she watched him march down the lane, anger in every line of his body, and she knew he would not leave it at this. He would be back and he would not give up until he had her answer.

In the yard she saw him saddle his horse, and soon the thunder of the hunter's hooves went past her window, drumming on until they eventually faded into the distance.

Again she collapsed on to the bed, lying dry-eyed, staring up at the ceiling. Had it not been for her father she would leave, go back to London, get away from Nick Diamond. She never wanted to see him again so long as she lived.

Her father returned shortly afterwards, came straight upstairs to the bathroom, and she heard him whistling as he washed.

Afterwards he would go over to Nick's for his evening meal. She would have to make her presence known because there was no point in him going there again, ever.

She waited for him to change and then met him as he came from his room.

'Sherril, my love, I didn't know you were here.' In the shadow on the tiny landing he could not see her face, not clearly, and it was not until they went downstairs that he caught a glimpse of her anguish. His eyes narrowed. 'You and Nick had a row?'

'What makes you think that?' she managed lightly, though there was a tremor in her voice that did not escape her father's notice.

'I can't think of anything else that could make you look so stricken.' He took her shoulders, compelling her to look at him. 'What's wrong?'

She shrugged, her lips grim. 'We've finished, that's all.'

'*That's all!* You say it as though it's of no consequence. My God, Sherry, the last time I saw you the stars were shining out of your eyes. As a matter of fact I can never remember seeing you so happy in your whole life, and now you calmly tell me the whole thing is off!'

He pushed her down on to a chair. From a cupboard he fetched a half bottle of brandy and poured her a glass. 'Drink this,' he said gently, 'you look as though you need it, and then you can tell me all that's happened.'

She sipped the drink, feeling its warmth course

through her veins, but it didn't help. Nothing could. Nothing would ever take away the numb feeling her discovery had left.

Her heart felt like a block of ice, as though she would never be capable of loving again, and the way she felt at this moment she didn't want another man, not ever. They were a deceitful species and she hated them.

Men and horses were the two things she wanted to avoid for the rest of her life.

Peter waited until she had finished her drink, then he took the glass and sat opposite. 'Tell me about it,' he said. 'I can't believe that it's anything so tragic— surely it can be reconciled? You look as though it's the end of the world.'

'I'd rather not, Daddy.' He would say she was an idiot, she knew that. 'This is between Nick and me, and nothing you can say will make me change my mind. You may as well get used to the idea that there'll be no wedding.'

'I think you owe me an explanation,' he said.

'Let's say I've discovered something about Nick that I don't like and leave it at that.'

Her father frowned. 'Nick's a fine man, I can't think of one thing you could possibly have against him. You'll have to do better than that.'

She looked down at her hands, at her ringless finger, touching the spot where it had rested only hours before. She had been so proud of it, it had staked Nick's claim on her, it was a bond between them—and now that bond was broken.

Her honey-blonde hair swung about her face as

e violently shook her head. 'No, Daddy, I can't ll you, you wouldn't understand.' He ought to, it as his wife who had suffered, but she knew he ouldn't. He did not see things in the same per- ective.

He sighed deeply, impatiently. 'Sherry—whatever is you can't bear it alone. If you don't tell me, en I shall ask Nick.' He rose and went towards the oor.

'Nick doesn't know,' she said quietly.

He turned, complete disbelief on his face. 'It's etting worse every second. Nick doesn't know ou've broken your engagement? It's ludicrous! Vhat game are you playing?'

'He's aware that we're no longer engaged,' she id bitterly, 'but he doesn't know why.'

'And don't you think he has a right to know?' emanded Peter, striving to control his anger.

She shrugged. 'Maybe, but I don't feel I can tell im.'

'Why, because you know he'll think it ridiculous?'

'He probably would,' she cried. 'You probably ould, that's why I'm not telling. But to me it's rave enough to warrant my not wanting to spend e rest of my life with him.'

Peter Martin sat down again, his head in his ands. 'I wish I understood you. I wish I knew what as going through your mind. You're not only psetting yourself, but me as well, and Nick. Do you ink that fair?'

It wasn't, she knew that, but how could she admit hat was troubling her? When the tragedy happened

her father had never once blamed the horse
Admittedly he had been shocked, and deeply upset
but he had said it was an unavoidable accident. Hi
wife could have as easily got killed by anothe
vehicle, and no one then would lay the blame on th
car. So what was the difference?

But to Sherril there was a difference—a big differ
ence. A horse was not an inanimate object, he coul
be controlled, so why hadn't someone done some
thing about it, stopped him before he kicked he
mother?

She did not stop to think how strong a horse is, an
that out of control there was little anyone could do

Her mother had been the dearest person in th
world, they had been more like sisters than mothe
and daughter. She had been able to talk to her, g
to her with any problems, knowing her parent woul
understand, would always see her point of view.

When she had died Sherril had felt as though par
of her was missing. She and her father had consoled
each other in their grief, but there had been one bi
difference. He had never blamed the horse.

She supposed it was because he had loved horses
worked with them all his life, but she herself ha
found it impossible to accept his point of view.

And the fact that she had now discovered tha
Nick Diamond had bred the very same horse mad
it a thousand times worse. All her old heartach
returned, intensified with the knowledge that Nic
had withheld this very vital piece of information.

The fact that her reasoning was illogical made n
difference. To her Nick was at fault, everythin

emmed from the moment the foal was born in *his*
able. Okay, he'd sold it, he was no longer the
wner, but if he hadn't brought the animal into the
orld——

She sighed: it didn't bear thinking about.

'I'm going to have a word with Nick,' said her
ther at last. 'See if he can throw some light on the
bject. I'm getting nowhere with you.'

He had gone before she could demur, not that it
attered, for Nick was as much in the dark. Let
em commiserate with each other, let them try and
uzzle it out themselves. Perhaps they would come
› with the answer. It didn't matter, she didn't care.
ne didn't care about anything any longer.

Suddenly the tears came, silent tears that coursed
own her cheeks. She sat and let them fall. Dusk
rned to darkness. Outside the horses called to each
her.

Damned horses!

Her father returned. He looked at Sherril, her
eeks stained, her eyes red rimmed and puffy. 'Bed
r you, my girl. I'll bring you a hot drink. You'll
el better in the morning.'

Would she? Would she ever feel better?

But obediently she got to her feet and dragged
erself upstairs. Peter brought her malted milk, and
scuits on a plate, sat himself by the bed until she
ad finished.

He kissed her brow and smoothed her hair, as he
ad when she was a child, then left her. Nothing
as said about Nick. What was there to say?

Sherril had thought that morning would bring

relief, that the shock would not be so great, that sh
might even be able to face Nick—because it wa
inevitable they would meet. But it was still there—
the hatred, the numbness, the loathing, the absolut
incredibility that he had kept this thing to himself.

She glanced at the clock. Almost ten. She ha
thought she would never sleep, and was surprised a
the lateness of the hour. But still she lay there. Wha
was there to get up for?

In the end, though, she did roll out of bed. Sh
washed and dressed like an automaton, dragged
comb through her hair, not really caring what sh
looked like.

In the kitchen she filled the kettle and plugged
in, heaped instant coffee into a cup and waited fo
the water to boil.

A sudden rap on the door made her jump, an
before she could move Nick pushed his way in.

'This time I'm not going until I get an answer
he said. His powerful presence dominated the tin
room. He stood tall and broad and unyielding, h
grey eyes riveted upon her.

She glared back defiantly. 'Like I said before
you'll wait a long time.'

'For ever if necessary.'

The kettle boiled and she filled her cup, addin
sugar and milk, sitting down with it in front of he
She did not offer Nick a cup and he did not ask, h
merely watched her with an unreadable expressio
on his face.

'I love you, Sherril,' he said. 'Doesn't that mea
anything?'

'I thought it did—once.' She stirred her coffee, ˻p˼sently watching it swirl round her cup.

'And you love me,' he continued in a low, tight ˻vo˼ice. 'So what the hell is all this about?'

Slowly she raised her eyes to his. 'What makes ˻yo˼u so sure that I still love you?'

Thick brows rose. 'Do you want me to prove it?'

The last thing she wanted was for him to take her ˻in˼to his arms. It was the perfect way for her to ˻w˼eaken. Contact with Nick was explosive, no matter ˻h˼ow harsh her thoughts.

She shook her head. 'There's no point. It's over, ˻N˼ick. It was nice while it lasted. Maybe I should ˻ha˼ve known it was too good to be true.'

He swore and pulled her up from the chair, sliding ˻hi˼s hands behind her back so that there was no ˻es˼cape. 'It still can be good, Sherril. God knows what ˻d˼amn fool notion is going through your head, but it ˻ca˼n be resolved. I'm sure of that. Tell me, please tell ˻m˼e.'

His eyes were pained, but it was nothing like the ˻a˼gony that ran through her. 'There's no point. It ˻w˼on't make any difference. Let me go, Nick, you're ˻w˼asting your time.'

'I have all the time in the world.' His voice was ˻h˼arsh and his arms became a rod of iron, imprisoning ˻h˼er against the rock-hardness of his body.

She could feel his heart beating wildly, he was as ˻te˼nse as a coiled spring, and she knew that he had ˻n˼o intention of letting her go until she gave him a ˻sa˼tisfactory reason for breaking off their engage- ˻m˼ent.

Contact caused the inevitable weakness of which she had been so afraid, and she steeled herself, repeating over and over in her mind that this was the man who had caused the death of her mother.

'I hate you, Nick,' she said, without realising that she had spoken the words aloud.

He recoiled, but did not let her go. 'That much I'd gathered, or at least that's what you tell yourself. I prefer to think that you still love me, that it's some trifling matter that's bugging you, which can easily be sorted out if you'll only bring it into the open.'

'*Trifling matter?* Would I be making so much fuss if that's what I thought?' She flung up her head and faced him. 'No, Nick Diamond, you can rest assured it's something quite momentous.'

Savagely he lowered his head, possessing her lips, ravaging her senses until her thoughts were not clear even to herself.

'You won't get anywhere this way,' she managed when he paused for breath, fighting her own instinct to respond.

'Won't I?' His eyes glinted ominously and he renewed his assault.

By the time he had finished her head was swimming and raw, primitive feelings were coursing through her body. But it wasn't love. *It wasn't.* It was nothing more than sheer physical attraction, and she could hold out against that.

It was agony to resist him, but by sheer cussedness she managed it, and when he let her go with an exclamation of disgust she sank to her chair, burying her head in her hands on the table.

She had thought he might leave, and was discon-
rted to see him still there when she eventually
oked up. She drank her coffee, avoiding his eyes,
ut with the uneasy feeling that she was not going to
cape Nick Diamond as easily as she had hoped.

It was a relief when her father chose that moment
return. He looked from one to the other expect-
atly, frowning when he saw their stiff, irresolute
ces.

'Seems like I was expecting too much,' he
umbled quietly. 'I could do with a coffee, Sherry,
there's any going.'

'Me too,' said Nick, and his eyes held hers for one
nse moment.

Sherril shrugged and switched on the kettle,
aching out cups, trying not to listen to Nick and
r father talking quietly. But it was impossible not
when they were discussing her.

'Any luck?' questioned her parent.

'None at all,' replied Nick.

'She's stubborn,' said Peter.

'You can say that again,' returned his boss.
'All you can do is keep at her.'

'I intend to.'

Sherril flared. 'I'm here, and I do have ears! Will
ou please stop talking about me!'

'Why don't you see sense?' said her father reason-
ly.

'Sense? What is sense?' she cried. 'Nothing makes
nse any more. The whole crazy world's going
pside down. I think I'm going out of my mind!'

The two men looked at each other and shook their

heads sadly. Sherril knew what they were thinkin
they thought she *had* gone insane.

She felt as if she had, but knew that it was on
temporary, that as soon as Nick got out of her sig
she would be all right.

He incensed her, she only had to look at him
think of her poor mother and that great damn
horse. How dared he breed horses like that! Ho
dared he!

But she had to sit there, suffer in silence until th
had finished their coffee. Nick kept looking at he
causing her to shift uncomfortably in her seat.

His eyes were accusing, hurt, perplexed. A co
tinual frown creased his forehead, time after time
raked his fingers through his hair.

'It's not my fault,' she wanted to scream. 'You'
brought this on yourself. You ought to have know
how I'd feel.'

Eventually they went, Nick turning at the door.
shall be back. You'll break down, in the end, ha
no fear. If you truly love me, as I think you do, yo
won't be able to go on with this.'

Her chin tilted determinedly. 'Then you don
know me, Nick Diamond.'

'I do,' he said, 'far better than you think. Ou
love is stronger than whatever is troubling you.'

She eyes him scornfully. 'I wish I had your co
fidence.'

'So do I,' he returned harshly. 'So do I.'

CHAPTER EIGHT

SHERRIL spent the next couple of weeks trying to avoid Nick. But it was difficult. He seemed determined to confront her whenever possible and she lost count of the number of times she told him that there was no point in his pestering her, that there was no chance of her changing her mind.

Each night she cried herself to sleep, each night she dreamt about Nick, except that in her dreams he still loved him, waking with a feeling of euphoria only to have it dashed when she realised what had happened.

Ultimately she decided that the only solution was to leave the Diamond stud. It would hurt her father, but that could not be helped. In the long run it would be kinder.

She made her plans secretly, not even involving Meg, who had proved a good friend during these past unpleasant days, not probing, simply accepting that Sherril would tell her in her own good time what had gone wrong.

Her only problem lay in getting away without anyone seeing her. She had had her case packed for several days before the opportunity arose.

Quite casually over breakfast her father told her that he was accompanying Nick to the races. 'I shouldn't be late back,' he said, 'but don't bother getting a meal, we shall probably eat out.'

Sherril pretended not to show much interest, n[ot]
wishing to arouse his suspicions. She had been [so]
quiet and lifeless since breaking her engagement tha[t]
she knew he would become wary if she brightene[d]
up now. And he might tell Nick—who woul[d]
undoubtedly put two and two together.

No way did she want him to stop her leavin[g.]
That he still continued to seek her out amazed he[r;]
she had expected him to give up long ago. But onl[y]
yesterday he had come to the cottage, walking in a[s]
was his wont, demanding to know when she wa[s]
going to cease her stupid behaviour.

'Not now, or ever,' she had told him determinedl[y.]
'We're finished, and the sooner you get it throug[h]
your thick skull the better!'

Inevitably he had resorted to attacking her d[e]-
fences in the only other way he knew how. Gatherin[g]
her into his arms, he said, 'Sherril, you're killing m[e.]
Can't you see that there's no point in all this?'

And the anguish in his eyes had been clear. H[is]
love for her had in no way diminished. A pang [of]
conscience smote her, which she resolutely pushe[d]
away. Nick Diamond deserved all he got; if it hadn[']
been for him her mother would be alive now.

'You may not think so,' she said tightly.

'Then why don't you tell me what's on your min[d?]
Let's solve this thing together.'

His body was warm and firm against her own an[d]
she was so tired of fighting that she longed to rela[x]
against him, give way to the tell-tale quivering insid[e]
her.

Against her neck his lips were hot and passionate. 'Please, Sherril. I know you're not immune to me, even now your body is giving you away. What is it? If I've done something then for God's sake tell me, don't leave me in torment.'

She shook her head; it was all she could manage, if she spoke she knew her voice would betray her.

In the end, as happened every time, he flung her from him in disgust. 'I wish there was some way of making you tell me,' he rasped. 'It would appear to be a case of who has the most staying power.'

She eyed him coldly, better able to defend herself once they were apart. 'Since you're on the losing end why don't you give up?'

'Because I love you,' he said. 'And I happen to think that's sufficient reason. One day I trust you'll come to your senses.'

'I'm perfectly sane,' she exploded. 'My only madness was in getting engaged to you in the first place.'

'You loved me, you still do, except that you have some idiotic notion that I've done something, though God knows what.' His eyes were pools of pain. 'I've racked my brains for a solution. I lie awake at night thinking about the incongruity of it all. Doesn't that mean anything to you, Sherril? Don't you care how I feel?'

Deep down she did care, though she wouldn't admit it, even to herself. His face had aged these last weeks, lines had appeared that were not there before, his eyes were shadowed, haunted, and his skin had a pallor in complete contrast to his normal ruddy complexion.

She had done this to him, and she was glad. *Gla*
Determinedly she shook her head. 'You can go
hell for all I care! Now get out and don't com bac
again. You're wasting your time.'

And she was wasting her breath. She said it ever
time, it made no difference. Day after day Nic
sought her out, whether it was here in the cottage c
somewhere out on the moors. He must watch he
every movement, she thought, because no matte
how she tried to avoid him he turned up when sh
was least expecting him.

But now there would be an end to all that. Sh
watched his Range Rover leave and then with he
bag over her shoulder and her case in her hand sh
set off.

The five miles to the main road took her longe
than she had planned, her case becoming heavie
with each step. All she could hope was that fat
would be kind to her, that she would not have t
wait long for a bus.

Her prayers were answered. Only minutes afte
she had got there a bus appeared in the distance
She signalled and it stopped, and seconds later sh
was on her way to York.

Once there she went straight to the railway statio
and as though this was her lucky day a train fo
London was already waiting at the platform.

But not until it had moved out did she relax. The
she closed her eyes and smiled to herself—the firs
time she had smiled since that awful day she ha
discovered the part Nick had played in her mother'
accident.

She had written to a flat-owning friend in London who had said she was welcome to stay with her for as long as she liked.

Sherril had thought she would be happy to return to the city, but as the green fields gave way to greyness, to houses and factories packed tightly together, she realised with a pang that she was going to miss the Yorkshire Dales in a way she had never imagined.

And when she eventually got off the train, instead of feeling relieved and lighthearted, as she had imagined, her spirits dropped even lower.

Running away was no solution. She should have told Nick exactly what was on her mind—not that there would have been any chance of a reconciliation, she despised him too much for that. But it would have eased her inner tension.

She had left her father a short note, giving him her address, asking him not to divulge it to Nick, and she knew he would respect her wishes.

He was eminently happy in his new job and her departure would not be so catastrophic as it would have been when her mother first died. He had needed her then, now he was quite happy on his own.

She took a taxi to her friend's flat and fortunately found her at home. Val welcomed her warmly, showed her where she was to sleep, allowed her to wash and change, then said, 'Now suppose you tell me what this is all about. One day I receive an ecstatic letter saying you're engaged, and then a cry for help. What happened?'

Sherril could see no harm in telling Val; after all she was never likely to meet Nick.

When she had finished Val said, 'You're wrong you know, Sherril. Your mother's accident really had nothing to do with this Nick Diamond fellow. When he sold his horse that was the end of his involvement.'

'I know,' admitted Sherril sadly. 'But I can't help thinking that if he hadn't bred it in the first place my mother would be alive now.'

'It could have been any horse,' argued Val. 'Are you trying to say that you'd have attacked the breeder, no matter who he happened to be, rather than the owner for not having taken more care?'

Sherril sighed. 'I suppose not, but when I saw that photograph I went berserk, and no matter how much I tell myself that I'm being stupid I can't help it. I hate Nick Diamond and I never want to hear his name mentioned again.'

Her friend respected her wishes, and as the days passed Sherril became easier. She would never forget Nick, she knew that, she had loved him too deeply, but gradually even her loathing seemed to lessen. She could think of him without bitterness, although she knew she could never accept him into her arms again.

She managed to find a job and also took driving lessons, passing her test within a few weeks, much to her delight. Shortly after that she bought a car, not a new one, but it was sound and she enjoyed the freedom it gave her.

Her father wrote once a week, never failing to tell

ner that Nick still loved her and wouldn't she let
nim reveal her address.

On each occasion she replied that she never
wanted to see Nick again and it was about time he
accepted it.

In the end she ignored her father's news about
Nick and made no mention of him in her letters,
until at last he took the hint and Nick Diamond was
never discussed again.

Autumn came and went and soon Christmas
oomed near. Inevitably her father asked her to
spend it with him, and she put off replying for several
days because she knew it would break his heart when
she refused.

'Hey,' said Val one night, when she arrived home
from work, 'what was that fellow's name you were
once engaged to?'

'Nick Diamond. Why?' Sherril could think of no
reason for her to suddenly bring him into the conversation.

'He was in the paper today—wait a minute, I'll
find it.' Val delved into her bag and brought out a
crumpled newspaper, already turned to the appropriate page. 'Here, look, he's got engaged to some
American heiress, so she certainly isn't marrying him
for his money.'

Sherril's heart became leaden as she read the few
lines and stared at the photograph of Nick Diamond
smiling into the eyes of a beautiful brunette. He had
looked at her like that once, melting her heart, turning her legs to water.

'For an engagement present,' she read, Nick

Diamond has given his bride-to-be a colt which he confidently predicts will one day be a racehorse to surpass all racehorses. The colt's name? Lady Sherril, which, his fiancée said, she intended changing to Lady Ingrid. "It was named after one of his former girl-friends," Ingrid Somers was reported as saying. "Quite naturally I want no reminders of her." '

Sherril finished the article before flinging down the paper. 'He can't do that!' she cried hotly.

'Do what, get engaged?' asked Val. 'It looks like he has. Are you regretting giving him up?'

'I don't mean that,' snapped Sherril. 'He can't give her the horse. It's mine!' She was incensed that he had calmly presented the colt to his new girl-friend. 'I'm going up there,' she continued heatedly. 'He's not going to get away with this.'

'Do you think that wise?' asked Val seriously. 'I mean, his new girl-friend might object. Why not tell your father how you feel, see what he can do?'

Sherril sniffed. 'Daddy would never stand up to Nick, he respects him too much. He thinks I should too, but I'm damned if I'm going to sit back and accept this!'

She hardly slept that night, her mind active, highly indignant that Nick should act so callously. He could at least have asked her whether she still wanted the colt.

Early the next morning she set out in her little car for Yorkshire, but she had not realised how tiring the long journey would be. All her driving so far had been short trips in and around London, and before she reached half way her neck muscles were aching and her powers of concentration were dwindling.

She stopped at a motorway service area and drank several cups of black coffee. An hour later she felt refreshed and able to finish her journey.

Even so she could have sworn the trip was longer than when her father had driven them up several months ago, and the fact that she was tired did nothing to improve her temper. By the time she arrived at the Diamond stud she was fuming.

Parental love made her decide to see her father first, even though she would have preferred to deal with Nick Diamond.

She had opened the door and walked in before she realised he was not alone, but it was too late to back out. 'Who's there?' called her father.

When she popped her head round the living room door he bounced up. 'Sherry, my love, why didn't you let me know you were coming?'

She kissed him warmly. 'I didn't know myself until last night.'

Nick Diamond hauled his long frame out of the chair. For some reason he did not look as surprised as her father. He held out his hand. 'How are you, Sherril?'

'Quite well,' she said distantly, ignoring his hand. 'I believe congratulations are in order?'

He did not look as happy as she had somehow thought he might. He had lost weight, his face was gaunt and drawn, his eyes dull and heavy.

'You could say that,' he drawled.

Her father looked puzzled. 'What are you talking

about?'

'Nothing,' said Nick abruptly. 'I'll see you later, Peter. I guess you two have lots to discuss.'

Peter Martin was clearly perplexed, but for the time being preferred to talk to his daughter. 'How long are you staying?' he wanted to know. 'Is that your car?'

It was not until late evening, after they had caught up on each other's news, that Sherril remembered her real reason for coming. 'Can I go and see Lady Sherril?' she asked. 'I've missed her so much.'

Her father looked embarrassed. 'I'm afraid that's impossible, Nick's——'

'You don't have to tell me,' she cut in bitingly. 'I already had an idea, you've merely confirmed it. I'm going to see Nick.'

He half smiled. 'Have you changed your mind, Sherry, is that why you're here?'

'I wish I could say yes, Daddy. I know how pleased you'd be. But it's too late for that now.'

She waited no longer, going up to the big house, knocking on the door and walking boldly inside.

In the hall she shouted, 'Nick Diamond!'

He appeared as if from nowhere. 'Come in, Sherril. I've been expecting you.'

She followed him into the comfortable sitting room with its immense stone fireplace and chintz covered chairs. A fire burned brightly, cheerful and warming, making her realise how cold she was.

But the chill in her heart was not due to the weather.

'I'm glad you know why I've come,' she said flatly.

You can't give Lady Sherril away. She belongs to me, and well you know it.'

'You gave up all rights to the colt the day you walked out,' he replied grimly.

'That had nothing to do with it,' she cried. 'The colt was mine, and I demand that you return her!'

One eyebrow lifted mockingly. 'And if I don't?'

'I shall sue you,' she said calmly, though she knew he wouldn't.

'Sit down,' he ordered, 'and I'll pour you a drink. Then we can talk this thing over rationally.'

'No, thanks,' she replied shortly. 'There's no talking to be done. All I want is Lady Sherril, then I'm going.'

'Are you sure that's all you want? Are you sure there's no other reason for you turning up here?'

She glared. 'I can think of none.'

'Perhaps you need reminding.'

He approached her and Sherril backed away. 'I think you're forgetting that you're no longer a free man!'

'I'm as free as the air,' he said nonchalantly.

Her eyes snapped. 'Another short-lived engagement. What happened this time?'

'She wasn't the right woman.'

'So third time lucky didn't work for you. What a pity!'

'Don't feel sorry,' he said. 'I'm not.'

'You sound as though you never even loved her.'

It hurt more than she had realised to think that he might. Facing him now, looking into the depths of his grey eyes, she knew that she still loved him. That

no matter what had happened it did not reall
matter. Perhaps without realising it she had bee
looking for an excuse to return.

'Does it matter to you?' Nick asked. He stood onl
a few inches away and she could feel shock wave
vibrating through her.

Trying to appear unconcerned, Sherril shook he
head. 'Why should I care? You mean nothing to m
now. It's Lady Sherril I'm concerned about.'

'Suppose I got her back. What would you sa
then?'

Sherril tossed her head angrily. 'You're re
markably free with your presents. First you give th
colt to me, then it's handed over to your America
lover. What will she say, do you think? Won't she b
as annoyed as I am?'

His lips twitched. 'I don't think so. She understoo
the situation.'

Sherril had the feeling that he was hiding some
thing. She frowned, her green eyes puzzled. 'Suppos
you explain the whole situation. Who is Ingri
Somers?'

He smiled warmly, sending shivers through he
spine. It had been a mistake to come, she ought t
have realised she could not wipe him from he
memory so easily.

'She's a friend, a very old friend, and she was quit
willing to oblige.'

Sherril's frown deepened. 'Would you mind tellin
me what you're talking about?'

'It amused her to pose as my fiancée. It was un
fortunate that she had to return to America s

ddenly. She would have liked to stay and see the
utcome.'

'Pose?' Sherril sat down suddenly. 'So you weren't
ally engaged. Then why the notice in the news-
aper?'

Nick perched himself on the arm of her chair. She
rank back into the cushion, finding him too close
r comfort.

His face suddenly became harsh. 'When the girl I
ved took herself out of my life, and no way would
er father tell me where she'd gone, I had to do
mething drastic to bring her back.'

She stared at him unbelievingly. 'It was all a plan?
ou haven't really given away Lady Sherril?'

'Do you think I would?' Roughly he pulled her
p, clamping her against him so that she felt the
pid beating of his heart. 'You and that colt are the
earest things to me in the whole world. She's with
friend at the moment. I didn't want you discover-
g her first and ruining the whole carefully con-
eived plot.'

She allowed him to kiss her, she could not help
erself. It was all she had ever remembered, and she
ung to him hungrily, returning kiss for kiss, strain-
g herself against him.

It was a long, long time before Nick let her go.
he fell weakly back into the chair, looking up at
im wonderingly, fingers touching her bruised lips.

'Now what have you got to say?' he demanded,
anding over her, arms folded across his powerful
hest.

She shook her head, conscious only that if she

parted from Nick again her life would be devas-
tated.

'Damn you!' he snarled. 'Say you love me.' He
leaned over and gripped her shoulders. 'I know you
do, so say it, before I shake it out of you!'

Licking her dry lips, she said shyly, 'I love you
Nick.'

He groaned and knelt beside her chair, pulling
her forward so that she was in the circle of his arms.
'I was afraid I was never going to hear you say that
again,' he said, his voice still anguished. 'I've been
going slowly out of my mind, do you know that? I
even threatened Peter with his job to make him tell
me where you'd gone. You're lucky to have a father
like him.'

'I know,' said Sherril softly, and then before she
could stop herself, 'I'd have my mother as well if it
wasn't for you.'

He stiffened and pushed her away. 'What are you
talking about?' His eyes had become suddenly cold.

'You should know,' she said bitterly, her resent-
ment flooding to the surface once again.

'Has this something to do with your breaking off
our engagement?'

She nodded.

'God, I should have known!' Enlightenment
crossed his face. 'That job I gave you to do—the
horse was in that book. Oh, my dear Sherril, I'd
never have asked you to do it if I'd realised.'

He attempted to pull her up, but she shrank back.
He frowned harshly. 'You're not going to carry on
this stupidity?'

'I can't help it,' she said in a tight little voice.

'So for the rest of your life you're going to blame me for the death of your mother? If that's the case, Sherril, maybe you're right after all and we shouldn't get married. I don't think that even I am strong enough to take that.'

He turned his back on her and the tautness of his shoulders, the rigidity of his spine, told her that he was deeply upset and bitterly angry.

She realised that she must choose. She could either face a future without Nick—a black thought that caused despair to flood her heart—or she must push from her mind all thoughts of the horse he had bred.

But she could not forget that her mother had been killed as an indirect cause of his breeding!

Very quietly she eased herself up and let herself out of the house. She loved Nick, quite desperately, but she also knew that it would be impossible to erase from her mind the part he had played.

Her father was waiting. He looked up expectantly, but his smile faded when he saw his daughter's disturbed face. 'I guess things haven't worked out as I'd hoped?'

She shook her head. 'Daddy, did you know that Nick had bred the horse which killed Mummy?'

His brows shot up. 'Of course I knew, Sherry love. I've known all along. Surely you're not blaming him?' He looked as though he could not believe it.

'Don't you?' she demanded strongly.

'Of course not, it's a stupid way of thinking. I'd no more blame Nick than I would the driver of the vehicle. It was a very regrettable accident, but that's all it was, no one was to blame.'

Suddenly tears fell. He was right, of course. She had known all along she had been behaving foolishly; it was just that she had found difficulty in accepting it.

'I've been silly, haven't I, Daddy?' she sobbed. 'And now I think I've lost Nick because of it. He says he doesn't want to marry me if that's what I think.'

'Then tell him you've come to your senses.' Peter gathered his daughter to him, mopping her tears. 'He loves you deeply. He's been going slowly out of his mind these last few weeks. I've almost given him your address more than once. Don't be afraid to admit that you could have been wrong. Go to him now, before it's too late.'

It would be, Sherril knew that. Once Nick made up his mind that she would hold a lifelong grudge there would be no changing it.

They met half way and she flung herself into his waiting arms. 'Oh, Nick, I'm so sorry! I didn't mean it. I've been a fool. If Daddy doesn't care why should I? Please don't——'

'Hush, my sweet.' He placed his fingers over her lips. 'It's all over and done with. We won't mention it again. It's been a terrible nightmare that's best forgotten.'

He kissed her then, and she clung to him as though she never wanted to let him go. She had almost lost him through her own stupidity, and as she realised how close they had come to a final parting she began o shake.

Nick gathered her up into his arms and carried
er back to the house, depositing her on a chair
efore the fire. He heaped on more logs and poured
er a glass of brandy, standing over her until she
ad drunk every drop.

'We'll get married on Christmas Eve,' he said,
and we'll spend our honeymoon right here in this
ouse. We'll bolt the doors and let no one in and
pend all our days making love, to make up for the
ime we've lost.'

Sherril's cheeks burned as she saw the hunger in
is eyes. 'Whatever you say, Nick,' she said meekly,
nd she meant it. Diamond word was law around
ere. She should have remembered Meg telling her
hat.

She smiled suddenly, impishly. 'What would you
ave done if I hadn't seen your announcement in
he newspaper? And how did you know I'd come
ack?'

He grinned. 'I knew that if you wouldn't return
or me you would for Lady Sherril. She's missed you
oo, she went off her food for days after you'd left.
And as for what I'd have done if you didn't turn up,
intended raiding Peter's cottage, searching through
is papers until I found your address. It was a last
esort, though. Even a blackguard like me draws the
ine at prying.'

'Why didn't you include Daddy in your little plot?
could tell by the look on his face when I offered you
ny congratulations that he hadn't the slightest idea
vhat I was talking about.'

'And risk him warning you? Oh, no, Sherril m sweet. That was my secret. Mine and Ingrid's, and reporter friend who did an excellent job, I mus admit. I think we'll have to ask him to the wedding The papers will be buzzing when they discover I'v chucked Ingrid for a little nobody without a penn to her name.'

Sherril wrestled a cushion from behind her an threw it at him. 'It's not too late for me to back out Nick Diamond. You'd better watch what you say!'

He caught it adroitly. 'That's enough of that, miss I see I still have a long way to go to taming you.'

His eyes suddenly glittered. 'Remember that nigh you begged me to make love to you? That's when thought I was winning. I hadn't realised what a long hard battle was in front of me.'

'Why didn't you?' asked Sherril. 'And why wer you so cold the day after?' It was something tha had puzzled her often.

'I never intended making love, I simply wante to see how far you were prepared to let me go Afterwards I was ashamed of myself,' Nick admitted 'I had no right forcing you into such a situation.'

'You forced me into many situations,' she declare strongly, but smiling all the same. 'I lost count o the number of times you threatened me with m father losing his job if I didn't do as you said. Di you really mean it?'

His smile was all-encompassing. 'What do yo think?'

'I was convinced you did at the time, now I'n not so sure.'

He nodded, still smiling. 'It was the only way I could get near you. You seemed determined to avoid me like the plague. Besides, I wanted to prick your ego. You were a cocky young thing, not a bit like the mental image I'd built up before you came.'

'I suppose I was a bit rude,' she admitted. 'I'm surprised you had anything to do with me.'

'I could see through the ebullience,' he said. 'I knew that underneath was a gentle, warmhearted girl who would make me an excellent wife.'

'Such confidence!' mocked Sherril.

'Come here,' he said, and she went willingly into his arms. It was a long time before either of them spoke again. Then Sherril said, 'I suppose we ought to tell Daddy that we're—er—friends again.'

'Friends—and lovers,' said Nick and it sounded good.

Sherril smiled and nodded, burying her head into the comfortable warmth of his shoulder.

Best Seller Romances

Romances you have loved

Each month, Mills & Boon publish four Best Seller Romances. These are the love stories that have proved particularly popular with our readers — they really are 'back by popular demand'. All give you the chance to meet fascinating people. Many are set in exotic faraway places.

If you missed them first time around, or if you'd like them as presents for your friends, look out for Mills & Boon Best Sellers as they are published. And be sure of the very best stories in the world of romance.

On sale where you buy paperbacks. If you have any difficulty obtaining them write to: Mills & Boon Reader Service, P.O. Box 236, Thornton Rd, Croydon, Surrey CR9 3RU, England. Readers in South Africa — please write to Mills & Boon Reader Service of Southern Africa, Private Bag X3010, Randburg 2125, S. Africa.

Mills & Boon
the rose of romance

Fall in love with Mills & Boon

Do you remember the first time you fell in love? The heartache, the excitement, the happiness? Mills & Boo know–that's why they're the best-loved name in romantic fiction.

The world's finest romance authors bring to life th emotions, the conflicts and the joy of true love, and yo can share them–between the covers of a Mills & Boo

We are offering you the chance to enjoy ten specially selected Mills & Boon Romances absolutely FREE and without obligation. Take these free books and you will meet ten women who must face doubt, fear and disappointment before discovering lasting love and happiness.

✂------

To: Mills & Boon Reader Service,
FREEPOST, PO Box 236, Croydon, Surrey CR9 9EL.

Please send me, free and without obligation, ten Mills & Boon Romance reserve a Reader Service Subscription for me. If I decide to subscribe I sh from the beginning of the month following my free parcel of books, rece 10 new books each month for £8.50, post and packing free. If I decide no subscribe, I shall write to you within 21 days, but whatever I decide the fr books are mine to keep. I understand that I may cancel my subscription any time simply by writing to you. I am over 18 years of age.

Please write in BLOCK CAPITALS

Name_____

Address_____

_____

_____

_____ Post Code_____

Offer applies in the UK only. Overseas send for details.

SEND NO MONEY–TAKE NO RISKS   XR2